## *Dying to Get Published*

"A sprightly novel . . . It offers a word to the wise: Never thwart a mystery writer, published or unpublished."
—CAROLYN HART

"Enjoyable reading for writers hoping to break into the mystery field."
—*Ellery Queen's Mystery Magazine*

"In a roller coaster of hilarity, Fitzwater has crafted three-dimensional characters with warmth, realism, and wickedness."
—*The Snooper*

"Fitzwater provides an entertaining (and for aspiring writers, frustratingly familiar) look at the world of writing and publishing."
—*Publishers Weekly*

"Expertly plotted . . . Ingenious and satisfying."
—*The Mystery Review*

By Judy Fitzwater
*Published by Fawcett Books*

DYING TO GET PUBLISHED
DYING TO GET EVEN
DYING FOR A CLUE
DYING TO REMEMBER
DYING TO BE MURDERED

# DYING TO BE MURDERED

**Judy Fitzwater**

FAWCETT BOOKS • NEW YORK

A Fawcett Book
Published by The Ballantine Publishing Group
Copyright © 2001 by Judy Fitzwater

http://www.randomhouse.com

Library of Congress Catalog Card Number: 00-110156

ISBN 0-449-00640-9

Manufactured in the United States of America

First Edition: May 2001

10  9  8  7  6  5  4  3  2  1

For my mother,
Bernice McGuire,
with love

# Acknowledgments

Writing is a solitary experience, one that takes a community of support. I am thankful for the many people who offer me their understanding, their advice, and their expertise, especially those whose names follow:

Larry, Anastasia, and Miellyn, who read this book so many times and in so many pieces I'm surprised they're still speaking to me.

Patricia Peters, my wonderful editor, who is as kind as she is talented.

Joe Blades, who is a delight to work with and whose support has been most extraordinary.

Robyn Amos, Ann Kline, Vicki Singer, and Karen Smith, who won't let me get away with anything.

Elaine Huey, who generously helped with part of my research.

Melissa Parlon, Bill Bickle, and Chuck Heurich of the Montgomery County Police Department for their knowledge and willingness to share it.

Please note: there is no Ashton mansion in Macon's historic district. It is a product of my imagination as is the Ashton family history and all the characters within these pages.

# Chapter 1

"A thousand dollars?" Jennifer Marsh pressed one ear shut with her thumb and shook her head as though to rattle it. Maybe that sore throat she had had last week had spread to her ears because she surely must have heard wrong. "I'm sorry. I thought you said some woman wants to pay me a thousand dollars a week to chronicle the end of her life."

An exasperated Monique Dupree let out a rush of air across the phone line. "That's *exactly* what I said."

Jennifer plopped down onto one of her dining chairs, the cord from the wall phone wrapping itself loosely around her neck and tangling in her long taffy brown hair. "What's the matter with her? Is she terminally ill?"

Cradling the phone between her shoulder and her ear, she let the last crust of jelly toast fall from her hand, back onto the plate. Absently, she brushed the crumbs from her fingers and pushed away her greyhound, Muffy, who seemed to think that maybe just this once Jennifer would let her eat from the table.

Jennifer obviously needed to give this discourse more attention than she usually afforded her conversations with Monique, which typically required no more than an "uh-huh" dropped strategically here and there.

"I wouldn't know what her problem is. The last time I saw her she did look a little pale, but she certainly didn't act ill," Monique told her, sounding miffed. "I agree it's nuts, but the woman is Mary Bedford Ashton, one of Macon's most prominent matrons. At least she was. She's slowed down somewhat this past year. Anyway, she's certainly got the money."

"What, exactly, does she want?"

"A straightforward daily accounting, sort of like a diary, as best I could tell."

"She could do that herself."

"I told her that."

"So why—"

"Why you?"

Jennifer gave in and tossed the last of the toast to Muffy, who was nuzzling her arm mercilessly. The dog caught it in midair.

"I'm not even a published writer," Jennifer reminded her. "Not yet anyway. With money like that she could hire almost anybody."

"She read about you in the newspaper. She knows you're a mystery writer, that we critique each other's work, and that you've been involved in solving some local crimes."

"What's that got to do with a diary?"

"I have no idea. She said she prefers someone from Macon." Jennifer could imagine Monique shaking her head. Mrs. Ashton had asked specifically for Jennifer when Monique was a published author, at least in science fiction.

"She's family, Jennifer," Monique confessed. "Her husband was my third, no, maybe fourth cousin removed I don't know how many times. He was a close friend of my parents. She asked if I'd contact you, so that's what I'm doing."

That explained a lot.

"Besides," Monique went on, "I know you can use the

money. I told her about Muffy, and she said you can bring her with you."

"Bring Muffy? Why would I need to bring my dog?"

"She expects you to stay with her in the house."

"Overnight? Oh, no, no." Jennifer was on her feet, heading, plate and coffee cup in hand, down her tiny slit of a kitchen to the sink. "I couldn't possibly. I've got obligations. I have my writing to do. And I have to help Dee Dee with her catering. She has two jobs already lined up for this coming Sunday and I've got an appointment Friday to give blood at the Red Cross."

"I thought you just did that."

"I give every two months."

"So one week, more or less, shouldn't make a difference. Just talk to the woman. It's a thousand dollars, Jennifer. How many turnip daisies and radish roses would you have to make to earn that kind of money? Need I remind you that you have bills to pay and that the small allowance you get from what your parents left you hardly covers your expenses? I don't know how you manage as it is. Food is a necessity."

"I eat," Jennifer insisted. "As a matter of fact, you interrupted my breakfast." She turned on the spigot and watched the crumbs disappearing off her plate in the stream of water. One piece of toast wasn't much of a meal, and technically, Muffy had eaten part of it. At thirty, Jennifer was overly thin and still lost weight easily, a fact that no doubt irked the fortysomething Monique.

Maybe she'd have another piece of toast if she could ever get the woman off the line. She might even scramble herself an egg. She rinsed her hands and turned off the water.

"How long does she need someone?" Jennifer asked.

"Who knows. She told me she didn't expect to last the week. She'll pay you up front, of course."

"Does she really expect to die?" Jennifer dried her hands on a dishtowel.

"Don't we all?"

Not really. Like Saroyan, Jennifer was hoping God might make an exception in her case.

"I don't know what her condition is," Monique added. "She sounded fine on the phone, but she seems convinced her demise is imminent. Meet with her. If you don't like her or her conditions, you don't have to do it. She's expecting you today at two o'clock."

"On a Sunday?"

"On a Sunday."

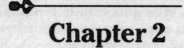

# Chapter 2

Mary Bedford Ashton, dressed in an ankle-length black lace dress, her copper-tinted white hair drawn back and up in a mass of curls, looked as though she'd been in mourning since the turn of the last century. She also looked quite asleep, lounging comfortably in a rose-colored wing chair, her double chins resting one upon the other, pressing against a beaded black necklace that appeared to be trying hard to contain them.

Without a word, the housekeeper turned abruptly and left Jennifer in the dark high-ceilinged sitting room of the Ashton mansion. Not a light was on, and although the heavy drapes of each of the four large windows were drawn wide, the room lay in shadowy darkness, stubbornly refusing to admit it was summer.

Jennifer smoothed the brushed cotton of her yellow calf-length sundress. She felt out of place, as if one had to dress properly just to enter that elegantly appointed room, let alone to speak to its occupant.

She cleared her throat. When she didn't get a response, she coughed as loudly as she thought polite. But Mrs. Ashton didn't stir, not even a detectable breath.

Maybe she was already dead. She'd give the woman five minutes. If she hadn't moved by then, she'd check for a pulse, have the housekeeper call 911, and get the heck out of there.

Even if the woman were only sleeping, as Jennifer prayed, the house was giving her the creeps. It was a magnificent antebellum mansion in Macon's historic district. Richly carved wood graced the arched door frames and wall panels of the spacious room. Persian carpets defined two sitting areas, and massive oil paintings, dark in color or with age, hung on each wall.

The effect was breathtaking, but more than just visually. The room had an aura of unease. It made her feel that something might be lurking in its shadows.

Careful not to step on the carpet, Jennifer lit on the edge of a stiff, velvet love seat designed more for show than for comfort and checked her watch. Four minutes and counting.

"Is she gone?"

The low, raspy words startled her. From where had they come? She and Mrs. Ashton were the only ones in the room. She squinted in the woman's direction. She didn't appear to have moved a chin, but in the dim light, Jennifer thought she detected the flutter of one eyelid.

"She who?" Jennifer asked. "I'm here."

"No, Melba. Has she gone?"

This time Jennifer saw Mrs. Ashton's lips move, ever so slightly.

She nodded vigorously.

"Good." Mrs. Ashton opened her eyes wide and pulled herself up, her extra chins disappearing in the process.

The woman had to be at least seventy, if not more, and undeniably overweight; but looking Jennifer full in the face in the dim light, her features soft and animated, her dark eyes catching what light there was, she was still beautiful. What must she have looked like when she was young?

"Monique Dupree told me you wanted to speak with

me," Jennifer offered tentatively, trying hard not to stare. "She said you wanted me to write something."

"That's right," the woman told her, the faintest hint of a lisp tugging at her words. "I want you to chronicle my final days, every single detail. You see, when I'm murdered, I don't want my killer to get away with it."

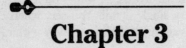

# Chapter 3

*Mary Bedford Ashton is crazy* was Jennifer's first thought. Her second was *I hope she's crazy*. Either way, the woman was not Jennifer's problem, and she intended to keep it that way. Still, she couldn't help asking one question.

"Who, exactly, wants you dead?"

"I can't tell you without your solemn promise to do as I ask."

"It's been really nice meeting you, Mrs. Ashton," Jennifer began, rising from her seat, "but I have things I have to do this afternoon. I must be going."

"Sit!" The word came with such force that Jennifer fell back onto her seat. Both women turned toward the doorway to see if anyone had heard and come in, but no one was there.

"Please excuse my outburst, Miss Marsh. It's such a pleasure to have you visit in my home," Ashton drawled in a softer, more genteel voice, a wide, artificial smile parting her lips. "Let me pour you some tea."

She pointed to the full silver service sitting on a table in front of her.

Jennifer didn't need anything she might spill, not in that house, and not at that moment. "No thank you."

"Very well." The woman's smile disappeared and she leaned forward with the indomitable will that only a

lady of the deep South can muster. It put Jennifer in mind
of her beloved grandmother. Such a sweet lady. Except
when Jennifer had done something wrong. Then it was
as though the heavens had broken open and the wrath
of God—

"I feel I know you already, my dear child," Mrs.
Ashton said. "Let's see. Your parents, God rest their
souls, died in an automobile accident when you were a
senior in college. Your dearest aspiration is to have your
mystery novels published, and to that end, you belong to
a weekly writers' group that has five members including
yourself. I also know that you're romantically involved
with Sam Culpepper, investigative reporter for *The
Macon Telegraph*. And I know that you have been in-
strumental in the solution of several crimes of murder
both here and in Atlanta."

"How could you know—"

"I read the newspapers cover to cover, both *The
Macon Telegraph* and the *Atlanta Constitution*, even oc-
casionally that rag, the *Atlanta Eye*. That's a lovely
photo they use in the *Telegraph* when they mention you.
A publicity shot?"

Jennifer nodded. That was Sam's doing, his way of
softening the blow whenever she got herself into trouble.

"Yes, it would be most appropriate inside the back
cover of a novel. Quite wonderful. And, as you know,
I'm related to your mentor."

Her mentor?

"Betty assures me you're quite talented."

"Betty who?"

"Oh, that's right. You call her Monique." Mrs.
Ashton dabbed at the corner of her mouth with a white
lace handkerchief. "She took on airs after she published
that book of hers, but she's always been just plain Betty
to me."

Of course. Monique had always been Monique to her, but her one book—published before Jennifer had met her—had come out under a pen name, and she had stubbornly adopted it. But Jennifer couldn't fault her. Left with the choice, she would have opted for Monique, too.

"As I was saying, Betty tells me that luck has simply not been with you even though you work tirelessly toward your goal.

"I'm not crazy," the woman added, apparently in response to the look on Jennifer's face, which, in truth, was a reaction to the comment about Monique's mentoring—she'd much prefer to think of herself as Monique's peer—and the obvious fact that she'd been talking about her. It had nothing whatsoever to do with Mrs. Ashton's mental state.

"If you're in fear for your life, you need to go to the police," Jennifer suggested.

"They won't listen to me. Dementia, they'll call it."

Jennifer would call it paranoia.

"I have no real proof, you see, nothing they could charge anyone with." Again, the woman leaned forward, this time conspiratorially, a note of desperation in her voice. "When I'm dead, I'm sure they intend to pass it off as natural causes. Well, I intend to see that they don't." She slapped the upholstered arm of her chair with such force that a tiny cloud of fiber poofed into the air.

Jennifer again caught herself looking toward the doorway to see if the housekeeper had heard that last outburst. Nobody was there, at least not that she could see. "You seem totally in control of your senses to me. I hardly think that anyone who speaks with you for more than ten minutes could be convinced otherwise."

"You're right, of course. But there have been extenuating circumstances."

"What kind of circumstances?"

Mrs. Ashton clucked her tongue. "Nothing for you to be concerned about at this point, but my credibility has suffered some damage."

"I see. Just what do you think the plan is? To kill you, I mean," Jennifer said.

The older woman shook her head. "I'm not sure. Quite possibly poison in my food or drink. Or the injection of some substance naturally occurring in the body, perhaps insulin or maybe potassium. Make sure they remember to check for needle marks, and don't let them forget to look between my toes and fingers. Those are easy to overlook.

"She might try drowning, I suppose," the woman went on. "I'm only taking sponge baths for that very reason, so if I'm found in the bath, it'll be a dead giveaway." She laughed, obviously pleased with her pun. "Or maybe she'll smother me in my sleep. I suffer from sleep apnea."

Jennifer gave her a puzzled look.

"I stop breathing when I sleep. Then I start up again—at least I always have in the past. The apnea's the best bet, I think. That's what I would do if I were planning to murder myself. A well-placed pillow and a little pressure . . . The doctor would never suspect a thing. And be sure, if it looks as though I've committed suicide, I haven't. One last thing—if I disappear, I didn't go willingly."

Okay. Ten minutes of conversation was more than enough. The woman *was* certifiable.

"So," Mrs. Ashton pressed, "I'll expect you no later than tomorrow afternoon. That should give you plenty of time to get your things together. I definitely want you here before nightfall. I'm more vulnerable at night. Pack what you need. You can go back for the rest later, during the day. Or we'll send out for whatever you forget. Supper is at seven. And don't mention any of this to Melba on your way out. I haven't told the staff yet that you'll be staying with us. I simply don't know whom to trust."

"I can't."

"Nonsense. Of course you can."

"I'd have to bring my computer."

"No computers. Nothing electronic. We don't want to tip anyone off as to what we're up to. Besides, we don't want anything that someone could access or distort. A plain, spiral-bound notebook will do. All entries are to be made in pen in your own writing. Oh, and make sure you get one small enough to keep on your person at all times."

"What about when I sleep?"

"Especially when you sleep."

"Even if I were to accept your . . . invitation, I won't be free before Tuesday."

Mrs. Ashton shook her head vigorously. "Tuesday might be too late. Come here." Her tone was such that Jennifer felt she had no choice but to obey.

Suddenly, the woman rose to her feet, which put her just under Jennifer's chin, and grabbed her hands. She stuffed a wad of hundred-dollar bills that must have been concealed in the folds of her skirt into Jennifer's palm and forced her fingers around it.

Jennifer squirmed. She hated taking money from a desperate person for something that seemed as if it should be a favor. But favors only passed between friends, she reminded herself. Besides, the woman wasn't competent enough to be handing out money, whether it belonged to her or not. And Jennifer hadn't yet decided to accept the offer.

"I can't," she protested again, trying to shove the money back into the woman's grasp.

Mrs. Ashton clamped an iron fist over Jennifer's hand. "Yes, you can. I certainly don't need it. How much do you think I can spend in the week or so I have left? Besides, I know what you're like, Jennifer Marsh. You're as transparent as you are idealistic." Her fingers pressed against Jennifer's flesh, her eyes steely. "If you don't help me, you won't be able to live with yourself, and you won't be able to do a thing when she kills me. You'll feel that my blood is on your hands. Can you live with that?"

Guilt was something Jennifer was well acquainted with. One way or another, she could find a way to make herself responsible for almost everything that happened on earth. But not this woman's death. She wouldn't let herself get sucked into that trap.

Still, Mrs. Ashton seemed genuinely afraid. Alone and afraid. But even if someone actually wanted her dead, would they go so far as to kill her? Wanting and doing were two entirely different things, as she well knew herself.

"I don't expect you to prevent my death, dear girl," Mrs. Ashton added softly, patting Jennifer's hand. "I'm hiring you simply to record the evidence of it. I'm not afraid to die. I almost hate to admit it, but I'm actually looking forward to it. But how dishonorable to be murdered and not have anyone know!"

"If I were to come stay here, and please understand that I'm not saying I will, this seems like way too much money."

Mrs. Ashton grinned at her, making no effort at all to disguise how foolish she thought Jennifer was. "I support the arts all the time. Why shouldn't you get the money directly instead of through some silly foundation that's only going to use most of it to pay the phone and the electric bills? Consider whatever you deem appropriate as payment and the rest as a grant. For your writing."

That made sense, but she still needed proof she wasn't about to take the woman's money for nothing. "Show me something, anything," Jennifer pleaded, "that would indicate you're in danger."

The woman looked stricken, almost betrayed. "You don't believe me."

"It's not that," Jennifer said, swallowing the "exactly" that tried to follow. "I just want to know if you have any evidence, something to work from."

"I have notes that I keep hidden. There was another one, just this morning. I think I put it in my pocket." Mrs. Ashton felt deep first in one pocket of her skirt and then in the other. "It was here, I swear."

"That's all right. I'll take your word for it."

"Then you do believe me." Fortunately she didn't wait for Jennifer to confirm or deny the statement. "Now hurry along. And don't be late for supper Monday. I think I'll have Arthur roast a chicken."

"I'm a vegetarian." Jennifer realized her consent even as the words escaped her mouth.

"I'll keep that in mind." The woman winked.

"And I can't make it for supper. My writing group."

"Of course. Betty told me you meet every Monday at seven. Very well then. Come in the afternoon and I'll have Arthur fix you a snack before you leave."

"That won't be necessary."

Suddenly, Mrs. Ashton put a finger to her lips, shushed her, and fell back into her chair, pretending to be asleep.

"But who?" Jennifer insisted, tugging at the woman's sleeve. "You didn't tell me who you think—" She stopped abruptly in mid sentence. Melba was standing at the door.

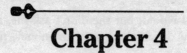

# Chapter 4

"Mary Ashton," Jennifer repeated. "Mary Bedford Ashton. You must have heard of her." She was leaning so far over that she was practically lying on Sam's desk, smack dab between him and his computer monitor, in his cubicle at *The Macon Telegraph*. She whipped her head in his direction when she realized no more letters were appearing on the screen after "Ash."

He raised an eyebrow at her.

"I'm in your way, aren't I?"

"Just a little."

He settled back in his office chair. The top button on his dress shirt was open, his tie pulled loose, his sleeves rolled to his elbows, and his dark hair teased one eyebrow. He was looking good for so early on a Monday morning.

He rested his hand on the small of her back, where her knit top brushed the top of her slacks, and watched her intently with those piercing, dark-blue eyes of his. She had to be careful of those eyes. He could make her forget why she was there. And he could read right into her thoughts.

"You're actually considering staying at this woman's house?" he asked.

He had a talent for cutting to the chase, which she appreciated—when it wasn't directed at her.

**15**

She turned the rest of the way around, leaned back against his desk, and looked him straight in the eye. "Don't tell me you wouldn't do it for a thousand dollars a week."

"Of course I would, but she didn't ask me, and I've never seen you do anything just for money, not even work."

That made her blush, not that she was ashamed, but because he knew her so well. And because she didn't want to tell him, at least not yet, that Mary Ashton feared for her life.

"She said her credibility had been compromised. I want to know how."

"Okay." Sam leaned over his keyboard, as Jennifer scooted out of the way, pulling up the side chair and confining her enthusiasm to a respectful distance. He finished typing in the woman's name and made a search of the *Telegraph* archives.

"Looks like we've got something from about eight months ago. MARY BEDFORD ASHTON DECLARED COMPETENT." He clicked on the headline.

"A competency hearing? Brought by who?"

"Whom."

She would have made a face at him, but he didn't look at her. She watched as he quickly scanned the screen. "Her sister-in-law, Eileen McEvoy. I'll print you out a copy, but I don't think you're going to get much out of it. Looks like her attorney was successful in having the records sealed."

"At least it's something."

He moved the mouse and clicked again. "I've got something else, an obituary. Look here. Her husband, Shelby Eliot Ashton, died almost a year ago at the age of 81."

She followed Sam's gaze as it traveled down through

the article. "He was quite a prominent man at one time, at least locally. He founded a number of charities. He also served as an adjunct professor of American history at Wesleyan College."

"So how'd he make his money?" she asked.

"By being born to it. And from investments, I'm sure. Says here his granddaddy was Willis Ashton. He added to the family's considerable fortune by getting involved with the paper industry around the turn of the last century. Must be nice to be rich," Sam mused.

"He isn't anymore," she reminded him. "Death is a great equalizer."

"So I've been told. I'll print the obit out for you, too. For anything further back, we'll have to hit the microfiche. You say she lives in the historic district, in one of those old mansions?" Sam asked.

"Right, not far from the Hay House and not all that far from your apartment."

"Some of those houses have secret rooms. They were used during the Civil War to hide valuables."

"And people. How, Mr. Culpepper, do you know all this?"

"I took the tour, you know, the one where you get on the little bus and the lady drives you around and tells you about the history of the area. Most informative. You ought to do it sometime."

She shook her head. "Those tours are for outsiders like you. I was born and reared in Macon."

"Right. Which makes you an expert. Want to catch some lunch later?" he asked, bending a little too close for office decorum. Lots of people were in the newsroom.

She blushed when she felt his breath on her neck and pulled back. They were already the subject of way too much gossip around the *Telegraph* offices. Word was there was a pool of bets on when or if they would get engaged, with dates ranging anywhere from next week to well into the next decade. When someone figured out their relationship, she wished they'd let her in on it.

"Wish I could, but I've got a lunch date with Leigh Ann."

She needed to get out of there. Mondays were always hectic at a newspaper, and she'd interrupted Sam right in the middle of a story. She didn't want to get him in trouble with his boss.

"Later tonight then?" he suggested.

"Nope. I've got writing group, remember? And I'm still wrestling with whether or not I should call Mrs. Ashton and tell her I've changed my mind."

"If this woman isn't competent . . ." He stopped short of warning her. He knew better.

"I know, I know," she assured him. "I promise I won't make any rash decisions."

"Now that would be a first," he mumbled, but she heard it all the same. That comment wasn't fair, and he knew it, but he just couldn't help himself. Whenever he got a little too close to perfect, he had to remind her he wasn't.

"I'll call you," she told him. "I'll pick up the copies from the printer on my way out." She pulled her purse off the chair, slung it over her shoulder, and paused at the doorway. "Thanks. I didn't mean to take up so much of your morning."

"No problem. I'll put it on your tab."

She'd really rather he didn't. She'd never be able to pay him back all she owed him as it was.

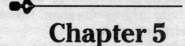

# Chapter 5

"So are you going to do it?" Leigh Ann asked from across the table at Ryan's Steak House. She was holding a fork stabbed through what would be a huge bite of greens. Salad was piled high on her plate, complete with cheese, croutons, sunflower seeds, cherry tomatoes, and who-knew-what under an embarrassing amount of ranch dressing. "Wow! I'd love to have the chance to stay on the Ashton estate. It's so, so, so—"

"Gothic?" Jennifer supplied. It had looked stately, the epitome of Southern heritage, right up until she had climbed those broad stone steps, stood next to those tall white columns, and set foot past the heavy, ornate doors. Then a chill had settled over her. For all its glorious marble flooring and gold leaf accenting the ceiling, she might as well have been in a house in Derry, Maine.

"Of course it's not Gothic. It's grand. It's majestic. It's—"

"Creepy," Jennifer finished. She swallowed a sip of sweetened iced tea and pushed at her own salad with her fork.

"Oh, pshaw. You're silly. It's just an old house. What do you think, there's someone locked up in the attic up-stairs?" Her green eyes suddenly grew huge in her petite face. "Oooooo. Did you see anyone who could pass for Mr. Rochester? Don't you love those dark, brooding

**19**

heroes? Jane Eyre's my very favorite heroine ever, even if she only had three dresses, at least to begin with. I never could relate to *Wuthering Heights*. It's always irked me that the critics say it's the better novel. What kind of future is there in being in love with a ghost? I mean really."

Ever practical, that Leigh Ann.

"No Mr. Rochester, no anybody really, not yet at least. Only Melba, the housekeeper."

Leigh Ann popped open a pack of captain's wafers, and crumbs scattered everywhere. She raked them into a little pile and then hid them between the salt and pepper shakers. "They're always the bad ones, you know."

"What are you talking about now?" Following Leigh Ann's thought process was like hanging onto the back of a downhill skier: tricky at best.

"The housekeepers. They always want their mistresses dead. Haven't you read *Rebecca*?" Leigh Ann rolled her eyes.

"You're not helping," Jennifer told her, more than a little unnerved. "I'd prefer you didn't talk about anyone wanting anyone dead."

"You're the one who writes mysteries," Leigh Ann reminded her. "So what does Sam say? You did tell him."

"Yes, I told him. He helped me look up Mrs. Ashton."

"Raiding the files of the *Telegraph*? For shame, Jennifer, using Sam like that. If he were mine—"

"He wouldn't be yours. He's not your type." There had been a time when Jennifer thought all men were Leigh Ann's type, but she knew better now. The brooding artist—that's what rang Leigh Ann's bell.

"You're right," Leigh Ann confessed, "but I wish he was. Can't help but love that man." She shook her head and raked more dressing through her salad. "I tell you, Jennifer, you keep stringing him along, and one day, just when you finally realize what a prize you've got, some gal will have swooped down and taken him away. They don't wait forever, you know. Life's too short. Before you know it, you wake up dead."

Okay. Mrs. Ashton missed a real opportunity, not asking Leigh Ann to come stay. They seemed to be working off the same page, at least as far as the imminence of death was concerned.

"So what did you find in the files?" Leigh Ann asked.

"Not much. Mrs. Ashton passed whatever competency hurdles the court put her through."

"So she knows who the president is and what century she's living in. But you say her relatives disagree—not about the president or the century—but about her competency."

"Right. At least her sister-in-law does. She *is* a little strange, but living alone in that house would give me the willies, too. Her husband died not quite a year ago."

"That poor woman. Of course she seems odd, trying to adjust to a loss like that. I know it can be difficult dealing with people in those situations, but are you going to do it? I'd jump at the chance. Jen, the Ashton estate is on the ghost tour, for heaven's sakes. You don't get opportunities like this every day."

Leigh Ann dropped her fork with a loud clank back onto her plate. "Oh, oh, oh. Maybe that's what you were tapping into, their resident ghost. Maybe that's why the place gave you the willies. Wouldn't that be something if you saw a real, live ghost?"

"So it's haunted, too." Icing on the cake.

"Only a little," Leigh Ann assured her. "The Ashton family were the ones who took in Amy Loggins back in 1864."

"The Civil War heroine? I've heard about her."

"Who hasn't? When she got word Sherman had made it to Atlanta and might be coming this way, she dressed in her brother's clothes and sneaked off to infiltrate one of Sherman's camps, hoping to blow up his ammunition and run off his horses."

"Only she got caught."

"Right. They hanged her and left her for dead. Some slaves found her, cut her down, took her back to their cabin, and nursed her back to health. That's when they discovered she was only a seventeen-year-old girl." Leigh Ann shook her head, her voice choking ever so slightly. "Can you imagine? They say her fiancé had been killed just the week before."

"If I remember correctly, she did recover."

"Well, yeah, but her true love was dead. How sad is that? And she was never right in the head after the hanging, which may have been a blessing."

Oxygen deprivation. It could do a number on the brain. "So you say the Ashtons took her in?"

Leigh Ann nodded. "She lived forever. I think she finally died sometime during World War II."

"How do you know all this?" Jennifer asked.

"I read. There's a wonderful book all about the ghosts that haunt Macon."

"And I suppose the author of this book has some kind of proof that these ghosts he talks about are real."

"Oh, I doubt it. He probably just reports what other people tell him they've seen."

"And someone has seen Amy Loggins in the Ashton mansion?"

"Of course, or it wouldn't be in the book. They say she wanders the upper floors. I'm sure she's mourning her lost love, just like she did when she was alive. Oh, Jen, you've gotta go."

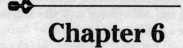

# Chapter 6

Two duffle bags and one vanity case later, Jennifer stood in jeans, a T-shirt, and sneakers on Mrs. Ashton's front porch. The summer afternoon sun warmed her back, as she held Muffy's leash tight in her hand. She'd give it a day, *one* day, she promised herself. Then, if she decided she couldn't do it, she'd return the money, which she had immediately deposited in the overnight slot at the bank on the way home yesterday afternoon. She'd felt like she had a neon sign on top of her little Volkswagen Beetle flashing: "Lots of cash. Come and get it."

Maybe she could get Sam to recommend a real journalist who did this sort of thing (whatever this sort of thing was). Or she could write a nice thank-you-for-your-interest note, suggest a good psychiatrist, go home, and get on with the book she was writing.

Muffy was playing wrap-the-rope-around-Jennifer's-ankles and pawing mercilessly at the bag that contained her food and treats when Melba finally decided to open the door.

"Yes?" she said, with a stern look down her nose. She glared first at the dog, who let out a soft growl, then the two bags and the case, and finally at Jennifer, who frantically tried to disentangle herself from the leash. Nothing like being tied up to put one at a disadvantage.

"Mrs. Ashton asked me to come. I'm to stay—"

"There must be some misunderstanding," Melba said, a wry smile twitching at her lips, her eyes ice cold. Her face was puffy with age, and her wiry hair was gray-white. She had to be almost as old as her mistress, yet she looked strong and able. Why was she still working? Didn't she have a retirement plan?

Jennifer opened her mouth to reply but was cut short.

"Oh, you're here!" a gleeful voice sounded behind the housekeeper. Mrs. Ashton pushed her way forward, her eyes glistening, her arms outstretched. She engulfed Jennifer in a huge hug and whispered in her ear, "Thank God."

When Jennifer drew back, she saw what looked like desperation mixed with relief flit across the woman's features. What color were her eyes? Brown, green, gold? They seemed to change with every blink.

By the time the woman turned back to Melba, all trace of anxiety was gone. "Prepare Juliet's room, Melba, and tell Arthur to fix an early supper for one. Jennifer won't be able to eat dinner with the rest of us tonight. Isn't it delightful? We have a guest!"

The straps of the bags had left huge indentations in each of Jennifer's shoulders by the time she struggled up the grand staircase, following Melba to the third floor. The woman hadn't even offered to help with the vanity case.

Then Jennifer had to go back downstairs, track down Muffy, who was exploring the brocade drapes in the sitting room, and coax her up every stair. She had no intention of leaving her dog to roam unattended on the ground floor and to slobber on priceless antiques. Or to find herself at the mercy of anyone or anything that might inhabit the house.

A large, worn, round sofa that looked as though it

might have been original to the house sat on the open third-floor landing, between the doors of the back two rooms that faced each other across the common area. Two wide stained-glass windows let in light that mottled one wall and part of the floor with rainbow colors.

Waiting not so patiently for Jennifer to struggle up the last steps with Muffy, Melba pulled open the door to the room in the far corner on the right. "This is Juliet's room."

Immediately Jennifer sensed something wasn't right. "Don't most bedroom doors open in?" she asked.

"It was necessary that this door be changed," Melba stated.

"Why?" Jennifer asked. If Melba wasn't going to volunteer information, she didn't feel at all awkward about asking for it.

"This room originally belonged to Amy Loggins."

"The ghost?" Jennifer uttered the words before she had a chance to stop them.

Melba gave her a strange look. "She wasn't always a ghost, you know."

"Did you know her?" Jennifer asked.

Melba nodded. "I wasn't much more than a slip of a girl, but I met her a few times. My mother worked for the Ashtons. Amy was fine most of the time, but sometimes she'd become agitated, wring her hands, and start to fret. When that happened, she had a tendency to roam. That's why they had the door turned 'round, so they could bar it at night, to keep her from wandering off while they slept. They never bothered to change it back after she died."

Jennifer ran her hand down the outside of the door frame. It had been refinished, but the evidence remained, putty-filled holes where brackets once stood. It seemed barbaric, even if it had been for Amy's own good.

"You haven't ever . . . I mean, after she died, you didn't . . ."

"See her?" She leaned conspiratorially toward Jennifer as though to whisper in her ear and then said in full voice, "No."

Melba drew back and gestured for Jennifer to go on into the room, obviously ready to dispose of her and get on with her own afternoon work.

The room itself was huge, bright and cheery with old-fashioned ruffled organza curtains covering windows that ran from the tall ceiling down to white-painted window seats with large, fluffy pillows in pink gingham. Bright pink rosebuds and green leaves dotted the white crocheted coverlet spread over the high four-poster bed. A small tapestry-covered step stool stood at the side of the bed, which was too high for a person of average height to climb onto without help. Jennifer thought she'd never seen a more warm and inviting room, a haven amidst the brooding darkness of the rest of the house. A most unlikely place for a ghost to choose to inhabit.

"It's lovely," Jennifer gasped involuntarily as she let Muffy off the leash to scoot about the slick wooden floors. She slid into the braided cotton rug at the foot of the bed and then went about snuffling under the bed ruffle.

Obviously, Melba was not pleased with the idea of having an animal in the house. But, aside from an expression that looked as if she'd been tasting lemons, she kept it to herself. "I'll bring up fresh linen shortly," she told her, bending to straighten the rug. "You'll find the bathroom two doors down the hall on your left."

Jennifer nodded appreciatively, dropping her shoulder bag on the seat of the chair at the small writing desk.

Then Melba threw wide the large doors to the closet and pushed blouses and dresses to one side and then the other, forming a decent-sized space in between. "I'll bring you up some hangers, too. The drawers are almost all full, but I'll see what I can do about that later if need be. You'll find fresh towels and washcloths in the bathroom."

Melba crossed to the door and paused, one hand resting on the knob. She turned and raised an eyebrow. "Just how long do you plan to stay?"

"I'm not sure," Jennifer waffled, touching the framed snapshot of an attractive, smiling, tan young woman, sitting in the grass, squinting at the sun. Her dark hair was long and straight, parted in the middle and held in place by a beaded band around her forehead. She had on a halter top and cutoff jeans, and her right hand was raised in a peace sign. The photo sat atop the dresser, next to a tortoiseshell comb-and-brush set, a jar of peach blush makeup that had dried into layers, an inlaid jewelry box, and a dish of bobby pins. "Do you expect Juliet back anytime soon?"

Melba gave her a strange smile. "Mrs. Ashton didn't tell you?"

"Tell me what?"

"Juliet's dead." And with that she pulled the door shut. Jennifer could hear her laughter grow fainter as she walked down the hall.

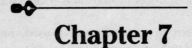

# Chapter 7

With her laughter, Melba had turned Juliet's beautiful summery room to winter. Even the sunshine that had poured brightly through the tall windows just moments before seemed to dim.

Jennifer knelt down, a shiver dancing across her shoulders, and Muffy scampered over to her, licking at her face and whimpering. She buried her face against the dog's neck, glad to have something warm and living to hold onto. "I know, I know," she soothed. "I feel it, too."

An almost imperceptible tap sounded on the door, and Jennifer scrambled to her feet, Muffy slinking behind her. Before she could speak, the door cracked, and she could see Mrs. Ashton peering at her through the slit.

"Are you decent?" the woman whispered. Not waiting for a reply, she slipped in, closing the door behind her, and leaned back against it. "You can't imagine how relieved I am to have you here. I received another threat, just this morning."

Maybe this wouldn't be the best time to bring up the fact that Jennifer wasn't wild about staying in a dead girl's room, especially one that was reputed to be haunted by Amy Loggins and that still contained all of Juliet's possessions.

"What happened?" Jennifer asked.

"When I awoke, it was lying on the pillow beside me,

28

written in bold red letters that looked as if they'd been made with a felt-tipped marker."

"What did it say?"

" 'You'll pay.' "

"That was it?"

"Yes. They're never more than a few words long."

"So where is this note?"

"I have it here." She pulled the folded piece of paper from her skirt pocket and handed it to Jennifer, who looked at it closely. The carefully formed block letters would be impossible for a handwriting expert to interpret. But the eggshell-colored paper was of heavy stock and was covered with a faint floral design in a light beige. It shouldn't be too hard to trace.

"Have you seen this stationery before?" Jennifer asked.

"Yes, of course. I bought some just like it some time ago. Then *she* had to have some. I know it's hers, but she'll say it's mine. Don't you see, that's how clever she is."

"Who *is* she?" Jennifer asked, certain she already knew the answer.

But Mrs. Ashton only shook her head.

"Was your door locked?"

"I keep it locked when I'm in my room and when I'm not."

So the house was insecure. Which meant her room, most likely, was, too.

"And you have no idea how *she* is getting in?"

"None."

"What, exactly, do you want me to do? Take this note to the police?" Jennifer asked.

"No, not yet. I want you to write it down, that I awoke this morning to that horrible threat, and yesterday's, and the day's before. I want you to record every unusual occurrence in this house, every strange sound, every intrusion. I want to get those notes to you before they somehow disappear. She won't dare do anything to you, I know it. Your sanity has never been questioned, has it?"

Jennifer shook her head. Not officially anyway.

"I have to have some sort of proof of these threats." Mrs. Ashton grabbed Jennifer's hands and squeezed, what looked like terror shining through her eyes. "Someone else has to see them, someone they'll believe. Promise me that you won't leave me alone in this house until we get to the bottom of this."

The threats couldn't be real. Someone must simply be trying to scare her. Society matrons weren't murdered, certainly not in Macon, Georgia. "No one is going to—"

"Fine. Then it won't hurt for you to promise, will it?"

Caught by her own words, Jennifer could have kicked herself. "All right then, I promise. I won't leave you until you feel safe. But I can't spare more than a week."

"Agreed, whichever comes first. Besides, a week should be all we'll need. And . . ." Mrs. Ashton paused, one eyebrow raised, waiting.

"And *if* you're murdered, which you won't be, I won't let them get away with it."

Relief washed over Mrs. Ashton. She was almost bubbly. "Having you here, in this room, well, you simply can't know what it means to me. I'm in the room directly below. It helps, more than you'll ever know, to think that you're just above me."

So that's why Mrs. Ashton had chosen Juliet's room for her.

"But you have to tell me," Jennifer insisted. "Who do you think is trying to kill you?"

Mrs. Ashton lowered her voice and leaned in close.

"My sister-in-law, Eileen McEvoy. She's never liked me, not from the first moment we spoke."

Mrs. Ashton walked over to one of the tall bedposts, turned, and grabbed it behind her back. She looked almost martyrlike, holding her head high and standing there like a suspected witch bound at the stake. "She did everything within her power to dissuade her brother from marrying me, and she's made it her mission on this earth to make me miserable. But there was nothing she could do. Shelby and I were meant to be together. He adored me."

"I'm sorry about your loss," Jennifer offered.

"Thank you, but don't concern yourself with it." Mrs. Ashton came back to Jennifer, grabbing her arm. "It's *my* death we have to deal with now. Eileen wants the house. And the money. To leave to her children. She says it's their birthright. She's been plotting ever since Shelby died. She'll do whatever it takes to get it."

"Even murder?"

"The competency hearing didn't work. Murder seems the next logical step. It's so final. No appeals, you see. I knew it was her immediately when the threats started coming. She grew up in this house. She knows every inch of it.

"She even told me," Mrs. Ashton added. "Outside the courtroom. She came up to me, took hold of my arm, and said, 'It's not over.' Then she leaned close to my ear and whispered, 'I'll get the house one way or another, over your dead body if need be.' How many ways can you interpret a statement like that?"

It seemed pretty plain to Jennifer, but people say things all the time they don't mean literally.

"I'll get the other threats to you later," Mrs. Ashton added. "You brought the notebook, didn't you, the one I asked you to purchase?"

"It's in my bag."

"Wonderful. Dig it out."

The woman stood over Jennifer until she'd retrieved the small book.

"Marvelous." Mrs. Ashton's eyes shone. "Now open it and record this morning's incident."

Jennifer didn't much care for someone standing over her shoulder and dictating her actions, but she reminded herself that she was being well paid to do exactly that. She scribbled the date and a few words, then shut it.

"Now put it in your pocket," Mrs. Ashton ordered, watching until she stuffed it in her jeans.

"I'm so pleased you're here to help me, Jennifer," the woman added kindly. "I can't do this without you."

Then she turned and was at the door before Jennifer could utter another word. She pushed it open the tiniest bit and peered out, seeming to search the hallway.

"Before you go," Jennifer called after her. "I want to know about Juliet."

Mrs. Ashton turned a steely eye in her direction. "I never talk about Juliet. Don't ask me again."

And with that she slipped back into the hallway, pushing the door shut behind her.

# Chapter 8

"Tell me about Juliet," Jennifer insisted. She was perched on a sturdy wooden chair in Mrs. Ashton's kitchen, which was located in the far back corner of the basement.

"Juliet? What you doin' asking me 'bout that girl? She was dead before I was born." Arthur Johnson lifted the pan off the heat, flicked his wrist, and the strips of squash, peppers, and onions flipped neatly in the air to plunge back into the sizzling olive oil. Jennifer could only stare. Except for Dee Dee and cooking shows on television, she'd never seen that done, at least not successfully, and certainly never that high.

"I'm staying in her room. All her things are there, and Mrs. Ashton won't tell me anything about her," Jennifer explained.

"Gettin' to you, huh?" Arthur dropped the pan back onto the fire and turned his brown, almost black eyes on her full force. He was probably a few years younger than she was, tall, well past six feet, with muscled upper arms straining in his white T-shirt, and skin as dark as richly finished mahogany. Gazing up at him, she thought he looked formidable. She wondered where she'd summoned the nerve to ask. Then his broad lips broke into an engaging smile, revealing perfect white teeth.

"What say I add a little chicken in with these veggies,

just enough to give them some flavor? I've got some marinating in my special lemon sauce in the refrigerator."

"Can't let you do it."

"I don't have none of that tofu stuff. Where you gonna get your protein, girl? What if I scramble you up an egg?"

"This glass of milk is fine. And you've already fed me a muffin."

"Muffins? Add that to this rabbit food and it still ain't enough to keep a bird alive. I'll put some pinto beans to soakin' tonight. You can have those along with brown rice and whatever I get together for Mrs. A tomorrow. Nobody's nutrition suffers when they're under my care. We'll see if we can't get some meat on those bones of yours."

"Juliet," Jennifer offered again, taking a bite of a second unbelievably delicious blueberry muffin. "You ever been in her room?"

" 'Course. I've been all over this house, used to play up there when I was a kid."

Jennifer threw him a look.

"My grandpap was Mrs. Ashton's cook. How you think I got this gig? He retired three years ago. I was just finishing my commitment to the service, and Mrs. Ashton asked me on."

"Which branch of service?"

"Air Force. Four years."

"Did you cook for them, too?"

He shook his head. "Med tech. Smoothest needle in my unit. Never took me more than one stick."

"Yeah? So why didn't you stay with it? They're in demand."

"You kidding me? I don't intend to spend my life 'round no sick people."

"I see. So you'd rather cook in a private home instead."

Arthur raked the vegetables onto a plate and handed it to Jennifer. Then he sat down across the stainless-steel table from her and helped himself to one of the muffins that sat in a basket. "Do I look like someone who would content himself with this?"

He motioned about the spacious state-of-the-art kitchen. It had four ovens, two sets of four burners each, two refrigerators with see-through doors, enough work space to pull in an army of assistants if need be, and two stainless-steel doors side-by-side behind her. She'd seen restaurant kitchens that weren't nearly as well equipped. Dee Dee would think she'd died and gone to heaven if she had a kitchen like that.

"Yeah. Why not?"

"Because it's not mine," he told her, leaning in.

"This is some setup." She took another glance around the room. "What's that?" She pointed at the solid doors.

"Those are freezers."

"They're huge."

He nodded.

"Just how many can you feed out of a kitchen like this?"

"How many you got hungry?" he asked, grinning.

Point taken. "But why all this equipment in such a small household?"

"Mrs. A liked her parties, yes sir. But all that's stopped now."

"Since Mr. Ashton's death?"

"Sort of. Not too long after that."

The competency hearing. Something like that could put a dint in one's social life.

"But you eat up," Arthur told her. "I didn't make that for you to let it get cold."

She took a bite of squash. It was to die for. "And I thought Dee Dee was a good cook."

"Dee Dee Ivers?"

Jennifer nodded.

"She's good all right."

"You know her?"

"I do some catering on the side."

"Really? I help Dee Dee out."

"Wait a minute!" He smacked the table with the palm of his hand. "You're *that* Jennifer Marsh. You do those fancy vegetable bouquets that Dee Dee has so many orders for."

She nodded. "That would be me. So we're competitors. What's the name of your business?"

"The Art of Good Food. Clever, huh?"

She grinned at him. "So you're the Art. Dee Dee's mentioned you. So why are you working in a private home?"

"Mrs. Ashton asked me for a five-year commitment when she hired me. I've put in three years." He abandoned the muffin, stretched out his long legs, crossed them at the ankle, and leaned back with his hands clasped behind his head. "I've got two more to go. It's sort of like signing on for the military. A little green up front as an incentive, I do my time, then Mrs. A sets me up with my restaurant. She lays out the cash. Part of it is her investment, the rest an interest-free loan that I'm to pay back as the business takes off. In the meantime, I'm developing my recipes, putting together my own cuisine, building my reputation with my catering gigs. I make her meals and she gives me full use of this kitchen. That way I don't have to rent one."

Jennifer nodded. Sounded like a good deal to her, but he had adroitly avoided telling her what she really wanted to know. "You're not going to tell me about Juliet, are you?"

"Oh, I can tell you all right. I just ain't so sure that

once you hear, but what you'll decide you really didn't want to know after all." He got up and pulled a milk jug from the fridge and refilled Jennifer's glass.

"If she's dead, why has her room been kept like that, with all her things in it?" she asked.

"That was her dad's doing. He was never quite right after she died, and he refused to let anyone move a thing. He insisted Melba clean it personally, once a week, change the sheets, as if Juliet might come back any day. Melba still does it, like clockwork, even though Mr. Ashton is dead. Habit, I guess."

"How long has this been going on?"

"She died in 1972."

"Goodness. How old was she?"

"Nineteen."

"How did it happen? An accident?" There were no good ways to die, but some were preferable to others.

"This is how my grandpap told it to me. He was the one who found her."

"Found her dead, you mean?"

"Stone cold." Arthur leaned forward. "Lying in the bathtub, naked as a jaybird, both wrists slit open, the water cold and red as cranberry juice."

She could see Juliet in her mind's eye, sunk back against one end of the claw-foot porcelain tub, her sparkling eyes shut, the ends of her long hair dipped in the blood-red water. Jennifer shuddered. *At least she hadn't died in the bed,* Jennifer mused, a truly selfish thought but one that might allow her to make it through the night in that house.

"Melba had come to fetch him, all out of breath. She knew Juliet had to be in there, but she couldn't get an answer when she knocked. The door was locked and she couldn't get it open. Grandpap had to break it in. That's the story I heard as a kid."

"Why'd she do it? Juliet, I mean?"

"Hell if I know."

"What do you know about her life?"

"He never said much more about her, not one way or t'other. If you want to know what she was like, you can look through her things, ain't nobody gonna know. All those peace signs, flowers, and hippie crap. I figure she was into drugs, at least marijuana."

So he *had* been curious enough to look.

"Not to rush you along, but I do have a full meal to finish preparing," he said.

Jennifer needed to get a move on anyway. She had to take Muffy for a walk before she left for her writers' group. She gulped down the last bite of squash and finished off her milk, then stashed the rest of the muffin in a paper napkin. It was far too good to waste, and she'd probably be hungry before bedtime.

"This grandpap of yours. What's his name?"

"Luther Johnson."

"Does he live around here?"

"Sure. Down on Log Cabin Drive. Why?"

"No reason. Just thought I might drop by to see him sometime."

He threw her a sly look. "So you plannin' to stay on a while?"

She shrugged. "I guess."

"Let me give you a little advice my grandpap gave me when Mrs. Ashton asked me on to cook for her: Do your job, do it right, but don't you ever sleep in that house at night."

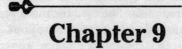

# Chapter 9

Thanks to Muffy, Jennifer was almost twenty minutes late arriving at Monique's house. Muffy hadn't liked the outside of the Ashton mansion any more than she liked the inside, so it took her twice as long as usual to do her business. Then when Jennifer finally got her back upstairs, gave her three treats, and shut her into Juliet's room, she whimpered so pitifully through the door, Jennifer almost didn't have the heart to leave her. Almost. Enough with the theatrics. One of them had to bury her yellow streak, and Muffy wasn't volunteering.

So the group had already begun reading when Teri answered the door. She shushed Jennifer and led her to her usual spot on the sectional sofa next to Leigh Ann, who grinned and drew up her short legs to make room.

Teri planted herself back on the floor on her tummy, arched her back in a most unnatural, serpentine fashion, and then rested her head on the palms of her hands. Jennifer pretended not to notice her staring up at her with a thoughtful expression playing on her almost exotic cocoa features.

She hadn't spoken to Teri since Monique had talked her into going to see Mary, and for good reason. Teri always had an opinion, one she never kept to herself. In this case, Jennifer knew exactly what it would be: was she out of her mind?

April waved from her spot on Monique's other sofa, her bright blue eyes shining in her pleasantly round face, and lifted a baggie in Jennifer's direction. She plucked something small and dark out of the bag, probably a chocolate-covered raisin. She used the raisin part to justify the chocolate and pretend it was nutritious.

April was a grazer, constantly foraging, constantly rationalizing. When she was pregnant, it was because of the baby, and when she wasn't, it was because of her metabolism. Now it was because she was nursing.

Little Colette was finally old enough for April to leave her for several hours. Poor Craig. Jennifer couldn't imagine anything worse than trying to distract a breast-fed baby who had never taken a bottle. Once she decided she was hungry, he had no options. Jon, their four-year-old, was just one more handful to add to the mix. And, of course, April refused to carry a cell phone. Group was her only evening out.

Jennifer shook her head at April, refusing the raisins, and carefully avoided Monique's gaze. She didn't want to give her an invitation to comment on her tardiness. But she shouldn't have worried. She stole a glance in Monique's direction. Her plain, dignified face was a blistery red, and it wasn't because of Jennifer's late arrival or some imagined slight over Mary asking Jennifer to stay with her. She was holding pages. She rarely read, and despite her unquestioned reign as the only published novelist among them, it obviously made her nervous. Insecurity. It was the bane of a writer's existence, so much so, it had even dared to strike Monique.

She began again. " 'Gor-roc thumped his brightly plumed chest and clicked his tongue in a long trill that danced out of the range of human hearing. He was summoning them, the Shades of Orithirium, the spirits of the dead, both those long passed over and those most recent.

Moments passed and then the air filled with them, thousands upon thousands of shadowy life-forms, graying the air, as though a fog so thick no one could see their own hands had settled over the group, blotting out all but the faintest light.' "

Ah, yes. Orithirium. The "dead" on that world dwelled only a thin dimension away from the "living" inhabitants. They could be summoned at will by a Caller-of-the-Dead. They couldn't speak to the living, only pantomime their thoughts and reactions, but they could hear the Callers. The shades had the ability to follow the Great Curve of Time and, if not exactly predict the future, show where the actions of the living were taking them.

Yuck. The thought of it made Jennifer shudder and question where her own actions were leading her. She preferred her dimensions well divided. And ghosts, friendly or not, completely out of her awareness. And out of the room she would be sleeping in that night.

Gor-roc, as she recalled, had suddenly become aware of his abilities camping late one night on a great battleground. Callers did not choose their ability. It came upon them unsuspected, when they happened upon a Thin Shell, a place between the dimensions where the separation, through the number or emotional magnitude of the deaths, had made the division even less defined.

*Doesn't anyone have anything else to read tonight,* Jennifer wondered, hoping Teri or April would wave their pages and insist they needed help right away, that it was imperative that they take their turns first. They all knew Gor-roc's adventure by heart, and it wasn't making for good bedtime thoughts.

Monique went on. " 'Covering their ears with the webs of their hands, the Thesperians fell to their knees, writhing in pain, as the first rising moon cast a red glow illuminating the fog of shadows—' "

"Excuse me." Leigh Ann sat up and raised her hand. She was a braver soul than Jennifer. Or stupider. She was breaking a cardinal rule: save all comments until the person reading has finished.

"I know I've asked this before," Leigh Ann continued fearlessly, "but aren't those actors?"

Was that a growl? Monique didn't growl. Or did she?

"I said Thesperians, not thespians."

"Oh, sorry. Must have heard you wrong. But don't you think those words are too close to one another? Every time you say it I get this mental image of a crowd of actors in gorgeous medieval costumes—lots of velvet and brocade, with laced bodices, ruffled shirts, and tights—right out of Shakespeare."

"They're green and lizardlike," Teri reminded her, peering at her with half-lidded eyes.

"Well, I know, which is exactly my point. That word simply does not conjure up a reptilian image. But maybe it's just me. Sorry. Continue."

If it were possible, the blush in Monique's face deepened. " '... the red of the moon turned gold. The trill stopped and a terrified chant rose up among the living, crouched in subservience. "Hail to mighty Gor-roc, Caller of the Dead." The second moon had risen and cast a blue-green glow ...' "

"Excuse me." Leigh Ann again. Jennifer put a warning hand on her arm, but she forged boldly ahead. "If one moon is glowing red, how could the other one glow—"

"They're not both real moons," April reminded her, tugging on a long, blonde tress. "It was in the other part. Monique didn't start at the beginning this time. Remember?"

Why had Monique dragged Gor-roc back out? It wasn't as if that book hadn't been to every publisher in the English-speaking world and most of the agents this side of New Zealand. Nobody was going to take it on. Not because it wasn't a good story—assuming the reader could relate to a nonspeaking, tongue-clicking alien hero—because it was. And not because it wasn't well written. It was simply because publishers and agents had already passed on it. Nothing short of changing the title, all the main characters' names, and most of the plot—which meant basically rewriting the whole book—and her name was likely to get it another look. Monique had said so herself. Yet she simply wouldn't move on. What revision was this? Sixty? Her first book had been published years ago, and she was desperate to sell another. But it wouldn't be this one.

"Let it go."

Monique dropped her pages in her lap, and Leigh Ann, Teri, and April all stared at her with a kind of terror on their faces. Oh, cripes. Had Jennifer said that out loud?

"What the hell's gotten into you?" Teri asked, rising up, sitting back on her heels. Under her breath, she added, "You got a death wish I don't know about?"

Jennifer pulled herself up. She'd said it and she couldn't take it back, so she might as well finish. "Monique, the best advice you ever gave me was to write something new when my Maxie Malone series didn't sell, even though I'd written two sequels. I still haven't given up on it, probably never will, but I doubt it'll be the first book I sell. And I know I can write other characters now. I've completed six more manuscripts to prove it. Gor-roc has done his thing with the Thesperians, and the editors don't care. You have a wonderful point to make only they're not going to let you make it, at least not with a Caller of the Dead. You've polished that manuscript to absolute perfection. What more can you possibly do to it? You're a wonderful writer, Monique. You have other stories to tell. It's time to give Gor-roc a rest. You need to move on."

Jennifer stared straight ahead at Monique rocking away in that damned rocker, not saying a word, not for at least one full minute, and held her breath.

Without breaking eye contact, Monique laid her pages on the floor. "So, anyone else have anything to discuss?"

It was horrible. She'd hurt Monique, hurt her in her most vulnerable spot, and that wasn't what this group was about. But it was also about honesty. Where was the line between the two?

"I do," April volunteered, as though they were, indeed, ready to move right along. "I didn't want to say too much before because I wanted to make sure. It's so easy to get your hopes up in this business and—"

"Spit it out," Teri demanded.

"I've been offered a contract."

Jennifer felt as though she'd been slammed up against a wall. Monique was no longer looking at Jennifer. They were all staring in April's direction. Had she heard right? A contract? It seemed like a mythical concept, like a unicorn. Did they really exist? Had April actually seen one?

"What with being pregnant and then having the baby and all, I kept putting off finishing that first book in the series, *The Case of the Missing Nuts,* the one that children's editor requested. Remember I told you about it? It's the one about eight-year-old Billy and his sidekick Barney, the flying squirrel. They solve simple little mysteries involving items a child might find in a yard— acorns, leaves, tulip bulbs, that sort of thing—and a trio of dastardly chipmunks.

"Well, I did it," she went on. "Every morning for the past two months I sat Jonathan down in front of *Sesame Street,* put Colette down for a nap, and I finished it. I sent it off two weeks ago. She called me this morning."

April sat there grinning at them, her blonde hair lying soft on her shoulders, one of the sweetest people Jennifer had ever met. No one deserved it more.

So why, for three seconds, did they all want her dead?

Then it sunk in. At last. After all this time, someone other than Monique was going to be published. Published!

Leigh Ann started the clapping, and they all joined in. Then they rushed her—Leigh Ann, Jennifer, and Teri—laughing, hugging, truly happy, tangling into one large giggling wad of arms, legs, and heads. The sofa tipped back against the wall with a thump.

Monique, who had remained calmly in her seat, cleared her throat. Loudly. The four-headed creature strained to look.

"Did you bring champagne?" she asked April.

"Can't. I'm nursing."

"Well, we can. I've got a bottle I've been saving since this group first got together."

"That should make it nicely aged," Teri threw in.

"You get milk," Monique told April, ignoring Teri. "The rest of us get champagne."

Jennifer made out Monique's comment, mumbled almost out of earshot as she led the way to the kitchen. "I need a drink."

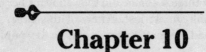

# Chapter 10

Jennifer never drank much. One glass of champagne made her woozy. More than that destroyed the filter that kept most of her thoughts from pouring right out of her mouth. Now they had toasted all the way to the bottom of a second glass. If they didn't stop soon, she'd be spending the night on Monique's sofa, or more probably, her floor.

"You could have mentioned the Ashton mansion had dead people in it before you sent me to stay there," she told Monique right in the middle of toasting Teri's future success, having already tipped one to Leigh Ann's, Monique's, and her own, not to mention a whole round for April's impending stardom.

Monique took the empty champagne glass from Jennifer's hand and set it in the sink.

She followed Monique, leaning over and whispering loudly in her ear. "And you conveniently forgot to tell me that Mary Bedford Ashton is totally whacko. Do you know Juliet's room is exactly like it was when she was alive? I understand that a mother—"

"Mary wasn't Juliet's mother," Monique said, setting down her own glass and turning to face Jennifer.

"But I thought—"

"Mary married Shelby sometime in the late nineteen-fifties, I think, could even have been as late as nineteen-sixty. Juliet was in elementary school. She was older than me by a year or two, but I vaguely remember the wedding. She was the flower girl. Her mother had died not too long before. I don't remember what from."

The fog cleared from Jennifer's brain just as Leigh Ann, April, and Teri sang out the chorus of "My Way" loudly and off-key. She wanted to shush them. Instead she leaned in closer toward Monique. "Mary told me she was the love of Shelby's life."

"If she was, he had at least one love before her: Juliet's mother, Clarisse. The only true memory I have of her is her voice, soft and musical. And the touch of her hand. So warm, so loving. She always hugged us—every one of the children who came to her home to visit—before she sent us off to play."

Jennifer saw the water rising in Monique's eyes, and she wondered if Monique hadn't had anything to drink, whether she'd be telling her any of this.

In the background, April hit a particularly discordant note and then dissolved in a fit of giggles.

"Her death frightened me," Monique confessed, rinsing Jennifer's glass. "I worried that my own mother might die."

Jennifer touched her arm. "That's a natural fear."

Monique offered a rare, shy smile. "My mother told me not to worry. Clarisse was in heaven, watching over us. I've never once doubted it."

"How could he replace her?" Jennifer asked, suddenly irrationally protective of a woman whom she'd never met and who had died before she was born.

"Mary certainly was beautiful. I guess he simply wanted Juliet to have a mother. He doted on that child. He gave her everything, including a baby-blue Mustang for her high school graduation. I was so jealous. God, I wanted that car." She scooped her glass back up and drained what was left. "That was one of my first life lessons. Don't envy anyone. Within six months she was dead."

"We're running out of bubbly over here," Leigh Ann announced. "What else you got?"

"I think there's a bottle of wine someone brought to the house last Christmas," Monique offered over her shoulder. "Look on the right in the back of the pantry."

"Juliet died from suicide," Jennifer said quietly.

"That's what they said."

"Were you close?"

"No. But a teenager doesn't have to know someone well for their death to affect her. She'd always been in my life, and then, suddenly, she wasn't. You say that room's been kept exactly the same all these years?"

Jennifer nodded.

"God. Who would have thought it? Juliet hated her."

"You're kidding. Why?"

"Maybe it was teenage rebellion. No, it couldn't have been. She never liked her, not from the moment Mary walked into their lives." Monique shrugged. "I don't know."

"Okay, got the wine." Leigh Ann declared. "Now I need a corkscrew."

"Try the drawer next to the refrigerator," Monique suggested.

Any effects the alcohol had had on Jennifer were now totally gone. Nothing like death to sober one up fast or to make one intolerant of other drinkers. "Do you know why Juliet killed herself?"

Monique shook her head. "She always seemed happy enough to me. Whatever she felt toward Mary, she adored her father and would have done anything for him. That fall she'd gone away to Auburn. She was back on break when it happened. Like I said, from where I stood, she seemed to have everything anybody could want: a loving father, a boyfriend who worshiped her, and more allowance a week than I could expect to see in a year."

"You're exaggerating."

"About the money? A little."

The phone rang. Monique excused herself and picked up the kitchen phone, said a few words, and turned to look at April, who was now dancing with Teri. They looked like they were doing some kind of cross between the Twist and the Running Man.

"Crisis on the home front," Monique announced. "Craig says if you're not home in ten minutes, he's bringing the baby here. I can barely hear him over the screaming in the background." She closed off one ear and listened intently. "He says she's been howling for the last forty minutes, barely coming up for air. He's threatening to divorce you and give you custody of both kids as soon as he gets over the operation for the damage done to his eardrums."

Again she listened. "Now I can hear Jonathan. He's hungry, too. Craig is telling him the water is boiling for the macaroni and cheese. Wait a minute. He's dropped the phone. . . . Hi, Jon. I know, sweetie. No, it's all right. . . . Daddy will get the water up off the floor. It only boiled over. . . . You stay back out of the way. He doesn't need your help. Your mommy will be home soon, and your dad will stop crying, I promise."

April already had her bag and was halfway out the door. She paused for a moment and turned. "You'd think a soon-to-be-published author would get more respect."

Monique sniffed. "Welcome to the real world, my friend."

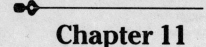

# Chapter 11

"Where have you been?" Mary demanded of Jennifer at the front door of the Ashton mansion. "I had no idea you'd be out half the night." She stood dressed in a pale green floral silk nightgown and robe, obviously ready for bed.

Jennifer checked her watch. It wasn't quite ten o'clock, hardly late by her standards. Besides, twenty-four-hour duty for seven days put $1,000 at just about minimum wage. Did she really expect Jennifer's full attention, every hour of every day?

The woman's expression assured her that she did.

She could, she supposed, blame her tardiness on Monique. After April left, she'd insisted they each drink three cups of coffee and walk heel-to-toe along one of the stripes on her linoleum floor before she'd let them drive home. As if Jennifer could ever do that.

"I'm sorry. Has something happened?" Jennifer asked.

"No, but Melba left over an hour ago. I had her take your dog out before she went, so you wouldn't have to go out again once you got home."

Locking the bedroom door, it seemed, hadn't made any difference at all. But then the key she'd found in her lock would most likely fit all of those old locks in the house.

Mrs. Ashton shut the front door and bolted it. Jennifer

watched as she punched in the security code and then checked to make sure all the alarms were set.

"I want all the evidence in your hands before another moment passes. I'll sleep much better knowing you have it. Come. Follow me."

Every light in the house seemed to be on. She led Jennifer up the stairs to her room on the second floor and pulled her inside, shutting the door behind them.

Did she actually think someone was somewhere in the house watching them? Jennifer caught herself checking behind her back, even with the door closed.

Mary's bed was covered in a natural-colored cotton comforter, and a matching lace canopy stretched between the bedposts. The room was elegantly in period, like something out of a museum, only without the burgundy ropes to keep visitors at a respectful distance.

Mrs. Ashton drew open one of the drawers of a massive old mahogany bureau, dug under her undies, and pulled out a manila envelope. "Take this," she ordered, thrusting it into Jennifer's hands. "Put it somewhere in your room. I've made a list of when and where I received each threat. It's in there with them. Now go."

Then Mary shoved her out the door, shutting it behind her without even a good-night. Jennifer listened as she heard the door lock click home. So much for all that glad-you're-here business.

Jennifer turned and faced the landing like a child put out of a car in a strange, unfamiliar place. Indeed, the ceilings seemed to rise even higher than they had in the daytime. There were too many doors, too many shadows, even with the lights on. She could almost feel the house heave, as though it had a life of its own, and it didn't seem to like her being there one bit.

Cautiously, she made her way around the landing

and then started up the stairs, holding tight to the bannister. At the first creak, she took off running, straight for
Juliet's room. How could she ever have left Muffy alone
in that place?

Muffy seemed none the worse for her outing with
Melba. She greeted Jennifer with slobbery enthusiasm,
then, wagging her tail, led her over to the bag with her
treats in it. Oh, for the simplicity of a dog's world. Right
now it'd take more than a liver treat to make Jennifer feel
better.

She gave Muffy two, rubbed her roughly under her
chin, and then carried the notes to the bed and carefully
shook them out. She took a comb from her purse and
moved them around, so she could examine and read each
one without disturbing any fingerprints that might have
been left by the sender. Although the way Mrs. Ashton
had toted the latest one around in her pocket led her to
believe any prints that might have been on them were
now long gone. All were on scraps of square paper of
varying sizes, patterns, and shades of eggshell.

Laid out like that, they looked almost silly, like something a child had done. Each had big square block letters,
all in red, spelling out trite phrases such as "DIE!"
"EVIL BEGETS EVIL," "IT'S ALL YOUR FAULT," and
"NOW IT'S YOUR TURN." But their juvenile simplicity made them even more unsettling. This was primitive emotion, not something that reason was likely to
touch.

*Why would anyone harass someone like that?* she
wondered.

To make them uncomfortable, afraid in their own home.

Well, if that was the intent, it was working and not just
on Mrs. Ashton.

Still using the comb, she scooted the papers into a pile

and then awkwardly managed to get them back into the envelope. *Where could she put them?* she thought, not that she really believed anyone would try to take them from her. But she was, after all, being paid to act as their guardian.

She took the small notebook that Mrs. Ashton had insisted she carry out of her pocket, opened it, and made a notation with the day's date: *10:17 P.M. Received from Mary Ashton the envelope containing threats. Took them to Juliet's room and hid them. . . .*

Her pajama pockets simply weren't big enough to hold the envelope without folding it. Besides, if she put the notebook in one and then added something in the other, she'd feel as if she were sleeping with saddle bags.

*. . . in the pillowcase with my pillow.*

She'd seen that done in some movie or other. At least if someone tried to take them, they'd have to wake her. She closed the notebook and put it away. Then she slipped the envelope inside the crisp white cotton case, replaced the pillow on the bed, and patted it. What kind of dreams would sleeping on threats give her?

She walked over to the chest of drawers and picked up the photo and addressed it. "So, Juliet, what do you think is going on here? Did you ever hate Mary enough to threaten her?"

Juliet's smiling image insisted that all she wanted was peace and love, man.

Jennifer set the frame back in its place and drew open the top dresser drawer. All of Juliet's things were there, seemingly undisturbed, as though the girl had simply stepped out to take her bath—a bath from which she never returned, Jennifer reminded herself.

In the second drawer, she found several pairs of cut-offs. She pulled out a pair and held it up to her waist, observing that Juliet had been small, thinner than she.

Next she inspected the legs. Jennifer was familiar with all the trappings of that era because her mother had also been a flower child. And what she noticed was a distinct difference between these cutoffs and the ones her mother had worn. The stitches that ran along the fringe suggested that Juliet's cutoffs had been professionally sewn. The tie-dyed T-shirt lying in the drawer likewise betrayed a professional look. Seems Juliet had gone down the flower child path only as far as her taste for expensive clothes allowed her. She was rebelling all right, but in style.

Jennifer put back the items, shut the drawer, and opened the inlaid jewelry box on top of the dresser. Love beads. Isn't that what her mom had called them? Jennifer pulled out one of the strands of brightly colored glass. The clasp had a brand name stamped on it. Why had Juliet adopted the appearance but not the philosophy?

She tugged at another strand but it seemed caught. One more yank and the drawer slipped out of the jewelry box. In the hollow where the drawer fit was a slip of paper and a photo. Written on lined paper, its edges ripped to fit the space, were two columns of names, four down each side. On the left were Andrew, Darren, Matthew, and Stephen. On the right were Caroline, Kelly, Mandy, and Tiffany. Darren and Tiffany were circled. Who were these people and why would Juliet have written their names and saved them in her jewelry box?

She set the paper aside and looked at the photo. It made her heart ache. The colors were faded but it was clearly Juliet, her hair long, either naturally stick-straight or ironed, and a blonde, long-haired, pony-tailed young man wearing John Lennon–style glasses with his arms possessively around her. They looked utterly happy, as though caught in one precious moment of joy.

On the back was written "Forever, Malcolm." Could this be the adoring boyfriend Monique had alluded to?

Lightly Jennifer touched the photo. *Dreams are so fragile,* she thought. *They never could have smiled that way if they had known her fate.*

She'd invaded Juliet's privacy, and, dead or not, Juliet still had a right to it. She started to slip the photo and paper back into their places and then stopped, pulling the picture back out and looking intently at it. The hair, the chin—they all seemed familiar, but how?

Malcolm. Malcolm Reed? Surely not. That scroungy scruff of a man who wrote "From the Other Side," a column for one of the city's free papers? But it would fit. The aging hippie still spouting his philosophy that the poor are victims of the state, that all injustice goes back to greed, that the government is the enemy.

The fire that had driven the hearts of so many of that generation had changed as the young rebels of the Sixties had settled down, had families, found their niche in society, and learned to work with the system rather than criticizing it, just as Jennifer's mother had.

But not Malcolm Reed. He'd become a lone, anachronistic voice, blind to how the world had changed around him. His passion still on fire. His indignation still driven by hatred.

Could he be Juliet's Malcolm?

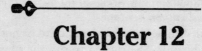

# Chapter 12

"I don't believe in ghosts," Jennifer reminded herself, pulling the crocheted coverlet tight under her chin and squeezing her eyes shut.

She really didn't. So why had it become an issue now? Because the place *was* creepy, no matter what Leigh Ann said, and ghosts sometimes seemed more real than flesh-and-blood bad guys. Hearing about Gor-roc and his calling up the dead hadn't helped either. Monique's scene of him lying next to a campfire and being joined by his father's shade was so effective that just thinking about it made the hair stand up on the back of her neck. She could understand why some clairvoyants cursed their gift. If she had it, she'd want to give it back, especially now.

The envelope Mrs. Ashton had given her crinkled every time she turned her head, reminding her, just in case she'd forgotten, that something terrible was going on, and it had nothing to do with who or what might be haunting the house.

She'd left the bedside lamp on, but it offered no more than a three-foot radius of light, only adding a second layer of shadow to the one already there and making it even harder to get to sleep, if that were possible. She could get up and flip on the overhead light, but that would mean getting out of bed. And giving up all chance of rest.

The whole house moaned as if shifting and creaking not only with age but with anticipation.

Muffy must have felt it, too. She lay in the center of the small pool of light, as close to the bed as she could manage, whimpering lightly in her sleep.

Jennifer would have let her in the bed with her, an absolute "no" rule in her own apartment, if the dang thing hadn't been so high off the floor. Well, they could both go home in the morning. She didn't need any of this: threats, ghosts, lost love, clammy sweats, sleepless nights. Mrs. Ashton must have someone in her life who could help her. She shouldn't be hiring strangers.

Jennifer buried her head deep in the fluff of the pillow and willed herself to sleep. Somewhere between the fear and the dark, she lost consciousness. She must have. Because when the screaming started, it brought her wide awake.

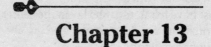

# Chapter 13

The first scream was a high-pitched sigh, like wind whistling through a canyon. It was followed by a blood-curdling screech. That one had her kicking her way out of the covers. No ghost had made that noise. It was a human, a human in pain.

Muffy, on her hind feet, whined and pawed at the side of the bed. Jennifer shoved her away, tumbled out of the high bed, and stumbled toward the door, not even taking time to get her slippers. She shoved back the lock, twisted the knob, and pushed. But the door didn't budge.

Another scream. This one followed by a low moan and then a "No, no, God help me, no." It was Mary's voice. Muffled and distant, but definitely Mary. It seemed to be coming up through the floorboards.

Jennifer rattled and turned the knob again, but the door stuck fast. She *had* to get out there. Why wouldn't it open? She made a fist and pounded desperately on the door. "What's going on out there? Someone help her!"

Muffy, in full courageous form, barked fiercely and scratched frantically at the bottom of the door, attempting to tunnel under it.

Jennifer put both hands on the knob and threw her shoulder against it. She bounced back and a piercing pain shot down her arm to her elbow. Nothing moved.

She ran her hand up the side of the door, feeling for

hinges so she could slip the pins from the inside, but there were none. The door did indeed open outward onto the hall just as she remembered.

Abandoning the door, she threw on the overhead lights and gazed about, searching the room. No telephone. Why would there be? No one had lived in that room for more than thirty years.

But her cell phone was in her purse, which lay on the chair next to the writing desk. Thank goodness she hadn't considered Mary's admonition against anything electronic to include her phone.

She grabbed the purse and dumped it open on top of the bed, scattering its contents. She took up the phone and flipped it on, frantically punching in 911.

"911 emergency. How may I help you?" a woman's voice asked.

"I think someone's being murdered," Jennifer gasped.

"What makes you think that?"

"I can hear screaming coming from the room beneath me."

"All right. Now I want you to stay calm. Where exactly are you?"

"At the Ashton mansion in the historic district."

"Okay. I'm sending someone out there right away. You need to—"

But Jennifer didn't wait to hear the rest. She dropped the phone on the bed.

She could hear sounds of movement in the room below.

She dashed to a window, climbed onto the seat, and peered into the dark. Muffy egged her on with little nips at her ankles as the curtains wrapped themselves about her shoulders. Frantically, she tugged at the lock. It probably hadn't been moved in years, and even if she managed to get it open, what could she do? She was a full three stories up from the ground with no convenient ledge or fire escape to crawl out on.

Finally the lock released and she pushed with all her might, raising the lower half of the paned window about a foot. She shoved hard against the screen, which tore loose and tumbled to the ground. It was a futile effort, but at least it was something. She put her head through the small opening and leaned out as far as she could.

Mary's room lay directly beneath. Looking down, she could see that a light was on, but little else.

"Mary," she screamed twice into the night, the cool air chilling her. Then she stopped, grabbed Muffy's muzzle to shush her, listened, and heard nothing. The house had reclaimed its brooding silence. She found it more terrifying than the screams.

Somehow she had to get out of that room, and short of bashing a hole in the wall, the door was her only bet. Again, she scanned the room, her eyes coming to rest on the items on the bed. A slender flashlight attached to her key ring lay under her billfold. She took it up and twisted it on. Good. At least the batteries weren't dead.

Bolting back to the door, she moved the beam to inspect the lock. It wasn't locked, so why wouldn't the dang thing open?

Dropping down on all fours, she flicked the light back and forth under the door. There it was. A shadow, about two inches wide, all the way on the left side, directly below the doorknob. Someone or something had put some kind of wedge under the door. What the heck was going on?

She couldn't let herself think about that right now. She had to get out. God only knew what was happening to Mary in the room below.

What she needed was something strong and small that would slip within the half inch of space between the door and the floor. Maybe a ballpoint pen would do. She always carried a steel one that had belonged to her father.

She scrambled up and grabbed the pen from the mess left on the bed, and then lay flat on the floor against the door, poking at the block. Her earlier efforts to open the door had only wedged it more firmly in place.

After several more painstaking and frustrating attempts, Jennifer finally loosened the block and jimmied it sideways. She stood up. Now for the moment of truth. She could only pray that whoever had blocked her in hadn't done something more to the door.

She attached Muffy's leash to her collar, wrapped it tightly around her hand three times, picked up the small flashlight, and cautiously opened the door.

She flashed the small beam about in the dark hall. After she'd gone to bed, someone had turned out all the lights. Except for an eerie hint of red that the moon cast through the stained-glass window, the area lay in gloom.

As best she could tell, no one was in the hallway. She had no idea where a light switch might be, and she certainly didn't have time to look for one.

She ventured silently, barefoot, into the hall. Amazingly, Muffy kept quiet. Alert and skittish, but quiet.

At the top of the stairs, she grabbed hold of the bannister, sliding her hand along the soft wood as she deliberately took each step down the stairs. A loud creak sounded, and she stopped to listen, but nothing below stirred. Then she continued, tugging a reluctant Muffy, who found these stairs difficult enough in full light.

At the second floor landing, Muffy let out a loud woof, her nostrils flaring, and strained hard against her leash, ready to make a run for it, but Jennifer held her back. They had to proceed with caution, not panic.

Nothing and no one were to be seen on the landing. They crept forward to Mrs. Ashton's door.

She wished she had one of those flashlights that could serve as a blunt instrument, one that took at least five or six D cells. Whatever she was about to walk into, she was unarmed.

Carefully, she grasped the knob on its side with the tips of two fingers. If there were fingerprints, she didn't want to disturb them. Then she twisted and the knob turned freely. A gentle push opened the door.

She stopped cold. Mary's room was totally dark. Someone had turned out the light between now and when she'd stuck her head out the window.

She whispered "Mary" as loudly as she dared. No one answered. Groping along the wall, her hand closed on a switch. She flipped it and light flooded the room.

Blood soaked the bed, so much blood Jennifer wouldn't have known what color the bedspread had been if she hadn't seen it earlier. It looked as though something had been butchered and bled out—right there in the bed.

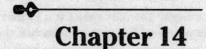

# Chapter 14

"How many times do I need to go over this?" Jennifer asked Lieutenant Nicholls of the Macon police. "It takes me longer to tell you than it did for it to actually happen. Let me make it simple: I heard screams, I called 911, I managed to force my way out of my room, I came to see what had happened, I found blood, and I went downstairs to wait for you to arrive. And I did not hear anything on the stairs, not before I left my room and not after. Have you still not found her body?"

"Not yet," Nicholls told her, "and we still haven't found the knife."

"Is that what you think was used?"

"Looks that way from the tears in the bedclothes."

Jennifer watched uniformed police and the rubber-gloved forensics crew crowding in and out of Mary's room, as she and the lieutenant sat on a forest-green sofa in front of the window on the second-floor landing.

One of the officers came over and nudged Nicholls. "We think a rug may have been removed."

"Yeah? Where?"

"There's a bare spot on the right side of the bed where a rug could have been. The bare spot doesn't have any blood, but there are flecks of red further out. And beyond those flecks is a smear of blood where a rug could have been dragged out a ways. My guess is they rolled the body up in it to take it out."

"Is that right? Should there be a rug there?" he asked Jennifer.

"I wouldn't know. The only time I was in that room was for a few moments before I went to bed. I didn't have time to look around. Ask Melba, the housekeeper. She'll know."

"She's next on my list." He turned back to the officer. "Did you find any blood on the stairs or the main floor?"

The officer shook his head.

"They probably used plastic sheeting," Jennifer offered.

Nicholls turned back to her, raising one eyebrow. "Think so?"

"If all that blood came from one person, the victim would have been sopping in it, especially if they moved her, which they obviously did. If they rolled the body off the bed and onto the rug, they could have pulled it, rug and all, onto the sheeting, wrapped it, tied it, and taken it down the stairs. Most other materials are porous and would likely leave some trace evidence. With the sheeting, there wouldn't be any blood outside of the room. I can't imagine any other way they could have done it. That would also explain why the blood was contained to only one side of the room."

"I see. You seem to know an awful lot about evidence."

"I write mysteries. Fiction. I'm supposed to know."

"A simpler explanation would be that you were involved."

Jennifer screwed up her face at him and let out an exasperated breath. "Don't even go there. You know I didn't do it. I called you, I have no motive, and, most importantly, I have not a drop of blood on me anywhere.

You'll find exactly two partial prints of my thumb and index finger on the rim of the doorknob and my prints on the light switch, and maybe on that wall. I groped around looking for it. I didn't touch anything else. You may find my footprints, although I doubt it because I took a sponge bath"—no way could she get in that tub— "before bed, and I didn't put on any lotion because I forgot to bring it with me. I freely admit to stepping into the room, as would anyone who heard what I did."

"Are you ready to come up for air?" he asked.

She drew in a great breath just to irritate him.

"Watch a lot of TV movies?" he asked.

"On occasion."

"We run into those every now and then, TV watchers, always trying to make things more complicated than they actually are."

"With no body and no weapon, I'd say you don't need me to complicate the situation."

"Right. Were you and Mary Ashton the only two in the house tonight?"

"Obviously not. But I thought we were when I went to bed. Melba had already gone when I got home for the evening. I watched Mary put on the security system."

"Well, it wasn't on when we got here. You say you couldn't get out of your room?"

"That's right. Someone put a wedge under the door."

"So you told me. Where is it?"

"It must still be upstairs, right behind the door where it was pushed when I opened it."

He shook his head. "We didn't find anything any-where on the landing area that could have been jammed under a door."

"But it was there. I swear."

"So you said. One last question. Why were you stay-ing here?"

As she talked, Nicholls had been scribbling notes in a small notebook. When she didn't answer, he stopped and looked up at her.

She had to tell him. "Mrs. Ashton was afraid for her life."

Nicholls cocked an eyebrow at her. "What does that make you, some kind of bodyguard?"

"What? You think I couldn't handle the job?"

That made him snicker. "Obviously not. Really, why were you here?"

"She wanted me to document what was going on, but I was only here the one night, and I didn't believe . . ." It was hard for her to even say it. How could she have been so wrong? "I didn't believe the threat was real. She told me she thought her sister-in-law was going to kill her."

"Name?"

"Eileen McEvoy. Mrs. Ashton gave me some threats she'd received." She pulled the small notebook out of the pocket of her pajama bottoms and handed it to him. "She had me write down that she gave them to me and about receiving the last threat this morning. That's the first entry."

Quickly, he flipped through the pages. "Where are these threats?"

"Upstairs. In the room where I was staying."

He closed his own notebook, put his pen back in his shirt pocket, and stood up. "Good. Let's go take a look."

Even as Jennifer slipped the envelope from between the pillow case and the pillow, she felt reluctant. Something wasn't right. If Eileen was behind this killing, she hadn't done it herself. Surely the savagery in the bedroom below could not have been the work of an older woman. Such women generally preferred poison, at least in mystery novels. And if it were a hired killing, why not a single bullet to the head from a gun with a silencer? This looked more like a thrill kill. But then how sane was a hired killer? And who said he was professional?

"Here," she said, offering the notes to Nicholls.

He took them, shook them out on the desk, and carefully looked through them, using a pair of tweezers.

"Mrs. Ashton told me at least one of those notes was written on stationery like some Mrs. McEvoy had purchased."

He grunted, and without a word, stuffed the notes back into the envelope and slipped it under his arm.

"They'll test that blood, won't they?" she asked. "For DNA."

"Yep."

"And they'll take samples in several places. If some of it's not—"

"What are you suggesting, Miss Marsh?" He was staring at her again. It made her nervous.

"Nothing. It's just that there's so much. . . ."

He smiled at her, a condescending, there-there kind of smile. "We'll take samples from several areas. In this kind of killing, the murderer is usually injured, either from his own hand or the victim's. He often bleeds. We'll be looking for more than one blood type."

Killing. More like slaughter. So Nicholls was certain Mary was dead.

"And you're sure it was Mrs. Ashton's voice that you heard scream?" he asked, one more time.

"I think it was. I heard it through the floor. I was sure at the time, but I don't know if I could swear to it now."

"Okay, Miss Marsh. I thank you for your time. Get dressed, get your things together—and your dog—and I'll have someone take you home."

"I can drive myself," she assured him.

He closed his hand over hers for a brief moment, just

long enough for her to realize it was shaking. "I don't think that would be a good idea."

He looked at his watch. "I'd like you out of here in ten minutes." He scanned the room. "All these items yours? You settled in pretty quick."

"They're Juliet's, Mrs. Ashton's stepdaughter. I only have the two bags and the vanity case." She pointed to them near the desk. She hadn't had time to unpack.

"Where is she?" he asked.

"She's deceased."

Again he raised an eyebrow. "You can come back tomorrow for your car, but I don't want you inside the house. We'll find you when we need you."

She nodded and watched as he let himself out the door. She waited a few minutes, listening to his footsteps retreat down the stairs, then pushed the door open all the way. No one was in the hall.

She heard voices drifting up the stairwell. Nicholls was interrogating Melba on the sofa on the second-floor landing. Jennifer crept to the railing and listened.

". . . and I left as soon as I'd taken that mutt outside."

"Was Mrs. Ashton expecting any company?"

"Not that she mentioned to me. She already had that woman staying here."

"Did Mrs. Ashton seem all right to you?"

"She seemed agitated, but that's not unusual for her. She's been that way since the competency hearing. Her sister-in-law tried to take control of the estate. This home has been in the Ashton family since it was built, before the Civil War. I can't believe that Shelby—that's her husband, Mr. Shelby Ashton—would have allowed control of it out of the family. He died last year intestate."

"That's hard to believe," Nicholls insisted, "with this kind of property."

"Shelby had a will, of course, but during his own illness, his lawyer, Mr. David Lambert, died and no one seems to know what happened to it. Mrs. Ashton insisted that Shelby had had it sent over from Mr. Lambert's office."

"Do you remember someone bringing the will to the house?"

"No. Mrs. Ashton said she received it personally and took it straight to Shelby and that he destroyed it, along with the copy he had here in the house. Then he died before he could make out a new one. That's how Mrs. Ashton got control of the estate."

"I see. We'll talk about all that later. What I need you to concentrate on right now are the events of this evening. Who knows the alarm system?"

"Just Mrs. Ashton, myself, and Arthur, the cook, but she could have shown anyone how to use it. It's not that difficult. All you need is the code."

"Could someone watching her put the system on at night pick it up?"

"Absolutely."

So Nicholls was willing to suspect Jennifer along with everyone else. As well he should. Even if he didn't think she'd participated in the actual killing, she could easily have let the killer in.

"If you ask me," Melba's voice again, a little higher and a little more disturbed, "you should be talking to that young woman she invited in. I can't imagine what Mrs. Ashton was thinking, letting a stranger like that into this house. She showed up one day and moved in here the next, just like that. You have to be careful who you let into your home. There's no telling what havoc they can bring."

"And you have no idea why Mrs. Ashton asked Miss Marsh to stay?"

"None."

Jennifer could imagine Melba's expression. Sour lemons.

She heard a flurry of activity as officers came up the stairs from the ground floor. Time was getting away. Nicholls had only given her ten minutes. Silently, she slipped back to her door.

She'd come out of that room for one reason, and it wasn't to eavesdrop on Melba's conversation.

She bent down and ran her fingers along the outside edge of the bottom of the door. A splinter caught in her index finger and she snatched it back. But she had found it. The slight indentation where something had been shoved beneath the door. Someone had blocked her in that room and then removed the evidence.

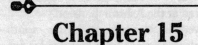

# Chapter 15

One of Sam's best qualities, and he had several, was that he never complained, no matter how badly or how often she inconvenienced him. That's not to say he didn't chastise her mercilessly when she'd done something stupid, because he did. But he was never more than a telephone call away.

When she got home to her apartment, dumped her bags, and let Muffy off the leash, the first thing she did was to dial his number. The phone rang before she realized what time it was: not quite six o'clock. He swore he was already awake, but she knew he wasn't. He seemed way too groggy, and he answered the phone with "Who died?"

For once, he got an answer to that question.

Within twenty minutes, he was knocking on her door. Although he'd forgotten to comb his hair and button one side of his shirt collar, he looked almost presentable. He held two large cups of coffee, wedged into a molded gray paper carrier, and a bag containing one sausage biscuit, one egg with cheese biscuit, and hash browns.

Sweet. Thoughtful. But grossly aromatic. In her current state, she couldn't face food or the smell of it, especially not the fast kind.

She pulled plates and mugs from the cupboard, unwrapped the sandwiches, and poured the coffee. She wouldn't have Sam drinking out of paper cups in her house. And then, sitting at the dining table, she let her biscuit grow cold while sipping the watery coffee and watching Sam devour his food as though no one had been slaughtered at the Ashton mansion.

He swallowed the last bite, wiped his mouth with a napkin, then blotted grease from between his fingers and took her hand across the table. "I didn't bring food over here so you could watch me eat, you know. There wasn't much else open. Can't you try at least one bite?"

She shook her head. He was trying so hard, but even the thought of food made her stomach churn. "Maybe later."

"Talk to me," he said.

She pulled back, stood, and taking her coffee with her, began to pace. "It looked like someone had taken a hose and drenched the bed, only not with water. If I remember correctly, the average human body contains something like eight to ten pints of blood. I'd say there had to be close to that much on that bed. How could someone bleed out like that?"

"Only a mystery writer would know how many—"

"That's not true. Anyone in the sciences or the medical professions, avid readers—lots of people would know it, too. Once the heart stops pumping, the blood stops flowing, so how . . ."

"They do it to cattle all the time," he interrupted. "They use a law called gravity."

God, what an image. It was one of the reasons she was a vegetarian.

"It's simply a matter of knowing where and how to . . ." Sam began.

She was right up next to him now. She leaned against his shoulder and put her fingers over his lips. She could pretend detachment, but it was a lie. She couldn't bear to think about what had happened to Mrs. Ashton. And, of all the people in the world who might tell her how it happened, Sam was the one she didn't want to hear it from.

He kissed her fingers, then took her hand and pulled her onto his lap, taking her coffee mug from her and putting it back onto the table. She wrapped her arms around him and hugged him as hard as she could, her ear and cheek pressing against his as though she couldn't get close enough, the stubble of his beard digging roughly into her skin.

And, then, for the first time since she'd awakened that night to screams, she cried.

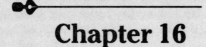

# Chapter 16

The doorbell rang repeatedly as though it had a short circuit. Who the heck would be at her door at eight o'clock in the morning? Sam had left almost forty minutes ago, and Jennifer had things to do, like getting the rest of her clothes on. She would very much appreciate it if whoever it was would come back later, if at all. Maybe they would if she ignored them long enough.

The door she could ignore. Muffy, however, was another matter. She bounced up and down like a rubber ball attached to a paddle, then stopped and let out a howl as though baying at the moon. Obviously the most important of Muffy's many and varied duties was door guardian. Unlike Jennifer, she really did want to know who was causing all that racket.

The bell sounded again, three times in quick succession. Jennifer pulled on a sleeveless cotton top over her jeans and shook out her hair, which was still wet from her shower. One more ding dong and one more howl and she'd have more than a few words for whoever was on the other side of that door.

Another ding and she was at the peephole, Muffy excitedly beside her. Leigh Ann stared back at her with a face so solemn she almost didn't recognize her. She barely got the door open before her friend pushed her way in.

"Did you see her?" Leigh Ann demanded, dumping her purse just inside the door. "Did you see Amy Loggins?" She was dressed in a long-sleeved blouse and dress slacks, obviously on her way to work.

Muffy circled both women, and after confirming it was only Leigh Ann, left to return to the bedroom, no doubt to sleep.

Jennifer didn't even try to hide her aggravation. "What are you doing here?"

"I heard it on the morning news—about the Ashton murder—while I was getting ready for work. I had to come by and check on you, and to find out if you saw her." She looked at her watch. "I've got at least twenty minutes before I have to be out of here, so give it up. *Did you see her?*"

"Thanks for asking how I am," Jennifer huffed.

Leigh Ann gave her a quick hug. "Oh, sweetie, I know you're all right. You always are."

But she wasn't. Not really. And if she didn't keep moving, didn't try to do something for Mary, she wouldn't be. But what good would it do either of them to share that with Leigh Ann?

"Amy must have been there," Leigh Ann insisted with the single-mindedness of a guard dog whose teeth were clamped onto an intruder. "If you're at all sensitive, and I know you are, you must have at least felt her presence in that house."

"Leigh Ann, a woman was murdered. I didn't have time for ghost watching. The blood . . ." Jennifer felt weak in the knees. She slid onto a chair and held her hands over her mouth. She couldn't let herself think about what she'd seen, not now, probably not ever.

Leigh Ann knelt down beside her. "You poor thing. You look white as a sheet." She disappeared into the kitchen. In a moment, she was back with a folded dishcloth soaked in cold water. "Here, put this on your forehead."

Jennifer took it and wiped her face. "I'm all right. I'm just exhausted."

"I know you are, and I wouldn't be pestering you about this right now except that people who have psychic experiences tend to talk themselves out of them. If you don't establish what happened right away, you may lose it entirely. Someone died in that house, and you were there. It's important that we record whatever you saw now, while it's fresh in your mind."

"I didn't see anything," Jennifer insisted, "that is, nothing supernatural."

"But you must have. It's all in there."

"In where?"

Leigh Ann went to the door, pulled a trade paperback book out of her purse, and thumped it soundly. "I looked it up again this morning. Amy Loggins has been dubbed Macon's Harbinger of Death. She's been sighted shortly before two deaths that occurred in that house, actually the only two before this book came out, that happened since her own death. I know the author is going to want to talk to you."

Jennifer dumped the wet cloth on the table, grabbed the book away from Leigh Ann, and opened it to the place marked with a scrap of paper. Leigh Ann had highlighted a whole paragraph.

" 'The first sighting of Amy Loggins was just prior to the death of Clarisse Ashton,' " Jennifer read aloud. " 'A neighbor'—notice, Leigh Ann, that this neighbor doesn't have a name—'noticed a strange glow, similar to something a lantern might put forth, flitting back and forth in the windows of the room that had once been occupied by the Civil War heroine. Ashton had been moved from her own room to avoid noise from the nursery while recuperating from her illness. That same afternoon Mrs. Ashton fell into a coma and was dead within forty-eight hours.'

"This is ridiculous," Jennifer insisted. "Of course there were people in Clarisse's room. The woman was obviously very ill. I hardly think they would have left her by herself."

"No, she wasn't. Read on."

" 'Mrs. Ashton, recovering from surgery as a result of a chronic gallbladder condition, had been left alone in the home for the afternoon, in the darkened room, insisting she would be fine without an attendant and requesting absolute quiet while she rested. No one was seen entering or leaving the residence until the housekeeper returned at five o'clock to find her comatose.' "

Jennifer shut the book and pointed at her with it. "This is such garbage, Leigh Ann. Nobody takes these books seriously."

Leigh Ann drew herself up and took the book away from Jennifer. "Maybe not you, but I think there's truth in it. The incident with her daughter's death is mentioned next." She opened the book and began to read. " 'More than a decade later, a strange phenomenon was again noticed by a neighbor walking his dog. A fluttering of light as though a lantern was once again moving back and forth in Loggins's room, perhaps searching for signs of Sherman's troops as Loggins was wont to do during her life, stopped the passerby. The house was completely shut down as Mr. Ashton was away on a business trip, his second wife was on holiday in Savannah, and Juliet was attending college. Upon her return home in two weeks, Juliet would be found dead in the house, a victim of suicide.' "

Jennifer was rapidly losing patience, her bout of weakness destroyed by a surge of adrenalin. "What would a ghost need with a lantern? And if she were searching for fires in the night, I very much doubt she'd need a light of her own. I suppose the next thing you're going to tell me is that Amy Loggins murdered Clarisse Ashton, Juliet, and now Mary."

"Of course not," Leigh Ann assured her. "Why would she? But I do think she knows when something is going to happen in that house, you know, like Monique's shades who can see along the Great Curve of Time. Are you sure you didn't see anything or at least sense her in that room?"

Jennifer grabbed up her keys and her purse, got a treat from on top of the refrigerator, and tossed it to Muffy, who had trotted back into the room as soon as Jennifer rattled the box. "Go to work, Leigh Ann."

"Geez, I was only trying to help."

"You want to help?"

Leigh Ann nodded vigorously.

"Then do two things for me. Drop me by the mansion so I can pick up my car, and find out who that neighbor is, the one who keeps tabs on the Ashtons. If we're lucky he or she may still be alive, assuming he ever existed at all."

"How?"

"I'd say you have two avenues. Contact this . . ." Jennifer twisted the book in Leigh Ann's hand so she could see the cover, "Douglas Wexler who wrote the book, or start knocking on doors."

"Really? Like a private eye?"

"Like a freelancer who's gathering information for an article for a newspaper or a magazine."

"You mean you think I ought to write—"

"It's your cover," Jennifer told her.

"Oh, I get it."

"But don't go alone. You shouldn't be knocking on anybody's door without somebody with you."

"I'll call Teri."

"Somehow I suspected you would. And don't do it after dark." Jennifer tugged her out the door.

"Where are you going," Leigh Ann asked, "I mean, after we get your car?"

"While you're taking care of the ghost angle, I have some flesh-and-blood people I need to talk to."

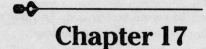

# Chapter 17

"I want to know everything you know about Mary Ashton's relationship with Eileen McEvoy," Jennifer insisted with her car keys still in her hand and Monique staring down at her, stone-faced, from the doorway to her house. It was barely nine o'clock in the morning. Jennifer noted a slight tremble in Monique's hand against the screen door and a twitch in the corner of her right eye.

"Jennifer. God, you don't know how relieved I am you weren't hurt. But this isn't a good time."

Monique was dressed but her clothes didn't match, and she didn't have on a drop of makeup. Dark bags puffed under her eyes. What time had she gotten the news about Mrs. Ashton? Who had called her?

"I'm not going away," Jennifer told her, shifting her weight back and forth on her heels. "You sent me over there. The least you can do is talk to me. You owe me that much."

Monique studied her, and Jennifer put on her best I'll-be-here-till-sundown look.

"I've already been on the phone with Eileen this morning," Monique said, holding the screen door wide for her to come in. "I'll give you time for one cup of coffee, but then you'll have to go."

She ushered Jennifer into her comfortably large kitchen, which didn't seem half as inviting as it had the night before. Monique pulled out a chair for her at the breakfast nook.

But Jennifer wouldn't sit down. Instead she followed Monique to the cupboard and stood right behind her while she took down a can of coffee and a filter. When Monique turned, she raised her hand. "Stop it, Jennifer. You're making me nervous. Go sit down." Then she added, "Please."

Jennifer obeyed, not because she had to, but because she could see that Monique was seriously rattled. She put away her keys and settled onto the wrought-iron chair, watching Monique fumble with the coffee grounds and then pour as much water on the counter as she did into the machine. She stood to help, but Monique shot her a warning glare, and she settled back down.

"I'm sorry I ever got you involved in all this," Monique said. She sopped at the water with a dish towel and then turned on the spigot at the sink and filled the carafe with more water. Not once did she look up. "I thought Eileen was right, that Mary was incompetent. I thought her fixation on her impending death was fantasy."

She shook her head, and Jennifer could see the muscles in the side of her neck contract. She must be choking back tears. Jennifer suspected she was out of practice at crying.

Monique cleared her throat. "I thought if Mary had a little company . . . She spent so much time alone in that big house since Shelby died. I didn't mean to put you in danger."

As difficult and holier-than-thou as Monique could be, she was fiercely protective of her friends. No one messed with them without answering to Monique, and she'd never knowingly hurt any of them.

"I know," Jennifer said. "It's not your fault. I talked to

the woman. I went there voluntarily. I thought she was nuts, too. I didn't come over here to bless you out. I came to get information."

Monique flipped the switch on the coffee maker and turned, at last, to face Jennifer. "You know how complicated family relationships can be. Feuds get started over nothing and seem to escalate beyond all reason."

Jennifer nodded. Her family had been too small to have a choose-your-side battle, but she'd heard about enough of them.

"I tried to see the good in Mary, and, who knows, if she'd been Shelby's first wife, things might have been different," Monique went on.

"Clarisse must have been a tough act to follow."

"She was. We all adored her. Mary had to be jealous, she had to feel she was second best, and I was never quite sure but what the resentment toward her wasn't based more in anger that Clarisse had died than in anything that Mary did."

Jennifer nodded. "You felt sorry for her."

"I suppose I did. She and Shelby seemed happy enough, at least until Juliet died. Mary was very active politically. She'd have meetings in her home. She'd tell us that the world was going to be a different place for young women like Juliet and me, that she was going to see to it. Of course Eileen was appalled, especially as Shelby let Mary have her way."

"Why? What was Mary involved with?"

"I don't remember, if I ever knew. At the time, I really didn't care."

Monique as a teenager. It boggled the mind.

"Change must be difficult for someone like Eileen," Jennifer said, "and I imagine it was hard seeing the Ashton mansion as a seat for political gatherings."

Monique frowned. "But it always has been. The man

who built it, George Washington Ashton, was said to be a secessionist who held secret meetings prior to the Civil War. People who have money don't just occupy their time spending it, you know."

"So when did the feud start?" Jennifer asked.

"It had always simmered, ever since Shelby married Mary, but when Juliet died there was so much guilt to go around. . . . That's when it hit full force with Eileen and Mary squaring off."

"And you've danced that delicate line all these years."

"I've tried," Monique assured her. "I guess I favored Mary a little only because she had so few allies. Eileen is so easy to like and Mary . . . Well, you met her. I can't believe she's dead, and who is there to grieve for her? It's so sad to die and have nobody care."

Jennifer went to Monique, but she drew back, wiping the tears from her cheeks.

"This is really important to you, isn't it?" Jennifer asked.

"Of course it is. Mary was family. We've got to find out who did this."

How was she going to tell Monique that the feud she'd just told her about may have been the reason that Mary died? "Eileen—"

"Eileen wants to talk to you. I told her I didn't think it was a good idea."

"To me?" She'd come there to demand everything Monique knew about Eileen, the woman Mary Ashton seemed so certain was behind her death. She never suspected Eileen would be interested in talking to her. "I can't. I'll be called as a witness. Mary entrusted me with threats to be delivered to the police in the event of her death. She said they were written by Eileen."

"I'm aware of all that, but Eileen hasn't been charged with anything, and, from what I understand, probably won't be. Those papers you gave the police were nothing. Besides, what could you say that could implicate her?"

A lot. Or could she? Now that she thought about it, everything Mrs. Ashton had told her would be ruled hearsay. She had no direct knowledge that Mary Ashton had ever been threatened. All she'd seen were notes that could have been written by anybody.

"I don't think the police can force you to keep away from her. She's a truly wonderful person, Jennifer." High praise from Monique who hoarded compliments like discontinued china patterns.

"She *may* have killed her sister-in-law."

Monique shook her head. "You'll never convince me of that. That incident at Shelby's funeral got blown way out of proportion."

"What incident?"

"I'd really rather not talk about it."

"*You* brought it up," Jennifer reminded her.

"It was all a misunderstanding, I'm sure. Eileen said Shelby told her and Mary the week before he died he wanted to be buried next to Clarisse and Juliet, but Mary made arrangements to have him put to rest on the other side of the family plot, where there was space for her, and then told the rest of the family that Shelby had never said any such thing. Eileen got angry and called Mary senile, incompetent, and worse, just plain mean. And then Eileen demanded to see Shelby's will, and Mary told her that he had destroyed it and hadn't made out another one before he died. Then she added exactly where Eileen could go."

"Whoa! So that's where the competency question came from."

"Right. Eileen insisted that Mary was either totally incompetent and couldn't remember what was said or she was deliberately ignoring Shelby's wishes. She even suspected Mary might have destroyed the will herself. She certainly couldn't get any satisfactory answers from the lawyer's office as to what happened to it. It seems to have simply disappeared."

"Heavy charges. Just how angry was Eileen?"

"She's not that kind of person, Jennifer. She's not violent. She's too much like her brother, Shelby. You would have liked him, too, at least when he was younger and Juliet was alive. He started to grow old the day Juliet died. If you talk to Eileen, even for a few minutes, you'll understand what I mean. She's one of the chairs for the Cherry Blossom festival, she's a member of the historical society, she's active in the arts. God, Jennifer, do you really think such a woman would commit murder?"

"We're frequently surprised by who is capable of murder," Jennifer told her. "If we weren't, none of us could sleep at night."

Monique shook her head, not in disagreement, but in despair. "I was trying to shuffle you out as fast as I could, but now I've changed my mind. Before you say another word to the police, the two of you need to talk. You won't understand until you meet her in person. She's on her way over here right now."

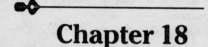

# Chapter 18

When Eileen McEvoy walked through Monique's door less than fifteen minutes later, Jennifer couldn't take her eyes off of her. If her calculations were correct, if this woman was Shelby Ashton's older sister, she had to be in her mid eighties. Yet she stood tall and straight, poised as though in control of every muscle in her face and body, her shoulders back, her head held high, her face timeless.

Every elegant white hair was immaculately and stylishly groomed, and she wore a cream-colored suit that showed she still had her slender figure. So cultivated, so Southern, so dignified.

And so terrified. But only in her eyes, intense and bloodshot. Her look was piercing.

She offered Jennifer her hand, looking down her aristocratic nose at her. Her skin felt soft. Whatever power she possessed had been seriously shaken.

"So you're the one," Mrs. McEvoy stated evenly.

"Excuse me?" Jennifer said.

"The one she chose to destroy me." Her lips trembled slightly as she forced them into a stiff, ironic smile. She dropped Jennifer's hand and took out a soft, white pack from her purse, fiddled with the cellophane cover, and drew out a cigarette. She offered one first to Monique and then to Jennifer, both of whom shook their heads.

"And you," Eileen said, addressing Monique. "You had a hand in this as well."

Monique paused in her preparation of a second pot of coffee. She and Jennifer had drunk the first one waiting for Eileen to arrive.

"I've tried my best to stay out of the feud between the two of you," Monique assured her. "I had no idea what Mary was going to tell Jennifer when she went over there."

"Well maybe you shouldn't have stayed out of it," Eileen told her.

"And just when did you start smoking?" Monique asked her. It was an obvious attempt to divert the conversation, but definitely worth trying.

"Right now. I stopped at Starvin' Marvin's on the way over. This will be my first." She popped the cigarette into her mouth, talking around it.

"First ever?" Jennifer asked.

"Ever. I've done everything right all my life," she told them, the lines deepening around her mouth as she flicked on a lighter, one of the cheap, disposable kind. "And look where it's gotten me."

Her face was flawless, her neck far tighter than it should have been. If she'd had a nip and a tuck here and there, she'd had a practiced surgeon. Not a scar showed.

She drew the fire into the tobacco, puffing only enough to get it lit. She didn't inhale. She looked almost ridiculous with smoke curling out of that refined mouth. If she felt like choking, she kept it, like everything else, well under control.

So this was how a lady of the South protested.

Monique came over and took the cigarette out of her hand, ran it under water, and dropped it in the sink.

"She used you," Eileen told Jennifer, studying her.

"How? By delivering the threats you wrote to her to the police?"

"Would you care to see a sample of my handwriting?" Eileen asked, pawing through her purse and pulling out a to-do list and a small address book. "Is this what the writing looked like?" She tossed them onto the table in front of Jennifer.

The words were all written in cursive, a flowing feminine hand. "The threats were done in block letters."

"How convenient. So all you have is her word, and we all know what that's worth. Did she say she saw me deliver those threats?" Eileen practically choked on her words, she was so indignant.

Jennifer shook her head, avoiding Eileen's eyes.

"She used you," Eileen repeated.

"Maybe she did," Jennifer agreed. "But she's dead all the same, and the police don't even know where her body is."

"You're assuming a lot. It's my understanding it will take a few days for the DNA results to come back. I wouldn't put it past that lunatic to have spread animal blood all over her room, just to see how we'd all react."

Obviously she hated Mary. Passionately.

"I heard her scream," Jennifer reminded her.

Mrs. McEvoy looked down at her hands, the only part of her that belied her age. She seemed tired. "I didn't wish Mary any harm. Not really. Not physically." Then she looked Jennifer in the eyes. "My children would have a fit if they knew I was here talking to you."

"Your children?" Jennifer began, looking over at Monique. Mrs. Ashton had mentioned them.

"Mark McEvoy and Stephanie Hyatt," Monique supplied.

Jennifer recognized both names. McEvoy was the head of one of the major construction companies in the area. He'd built a good number of the new homes in Macon. Hyatt was a well respected Bibb County judge. Until now, Jennifer hadn't made the connection. They had to be, what, at least fifty. It was strange to hear someone refer to them as children.

"You wanted them to inherit the Ashton mansion," Jennifer said.

Mrs. McEvoy fumbled through her purse. "Does anyone have a mint, something, anything to chew on?"

Monique handed her a stick of gum from a sweets bowl on her counter. Mrs. McEvoy unwrapped it and popped it into her mouth.

"Two years ago, when Toby died, she went on a chocolate binge," Monique explained. "How much did you gain? Ten pounds?"

"Fifteen."

"Was Toby your husband?" Jennifer asked quietly.

"Her dog," Monique supplied.

Mrs. McEvoy ignored them, intent on chewing her gum.

"The mansion," Jennifer offered again. Seemed she could never get anyone to stick to the subject.

Mrs. McEvoy looked Jennifer full in the face. "I never wanted the house for Mark and Stephanie. I wanted Juliet to inherit it, but that's impossible. That house has been in our family since it was built, and I want it to stay there, where its history will be preserved, where my brother wanted it and said so in his will that so conveniently disappeared.

"You have to understand what a vengeful, spiteful woman Mary Bedford Ashton was," she went on. "Whatever respect she obtained through the years was solely due to my brother's position in this city. He was so grief stricken over Clarisse's death, he couldn't see Mary for what she was. She slipped right into his life before he realized what she was doing. Once he did, it was too late."

"If it was all wrong, why didn't he just divorce her?"

"Shelby was a man of his word. He promised to stay with Mary. You young people wouldn't understand that."

"You might be surprised what we understand."

Eileen almost smiled. "Marriage was a commitment when he and Mary took their vows. And then when his daughter died, he just didn't care anymore. He and Mary may have dwelled in the same house, but he stopped living with Juliet's last breath.

"Is that coffee ready yet, Betty?" Eileen demanded. "This gum isn't doing it. If you won't let me have nicotine, how about caffeine?"

"It's coming," Monique assured her. The machine was still groaning.

"How did Shelby and Mary meet?" Jennifer asked.

"She worked for him, that's about all I know. Clarisse had that chronic gallbladder problem. She was so terrified of surgery, she wouldn't let them operate until it ruptured and she had no choice. It's a miracle she didn't die on the table. They kept her in the hospital for two weeks and then she needed extra help once she came home. Shelby hired Mary to care for her. She was a practical nurse, I think."

"Someone from one of the Atlanta papers called here this morning," Monique interrupted.

"Why'd they call you?" Jennifer asked.

"I helped Eileen with some activities for the Cherry Blossom festival. They probably got my name off the 'Net. They didn't seem to know we're related."

"So it's started." Eileen sighed. "That means they're probably harassing everyone I've ever known or worked with. Even the tabloids have the story—that she accused me of trying to murder her before she died." Eileen picked imaginary lint from the cuff of her jacket.

"How do you know that?" Monique asked.

"They keep calling the house. I unplugged the stupid phone."

"If you're innocent, your name will be cleared," Jennifer began.

"My name, young lady, is already ruined, simply by Mary's uttering it to you. Of course, I won't be convicted of anything. Do you honestly believe that a conviction is the only way to take one's life away?"

She was right. Whatever the outcome, the question would linger as long as the crime remained unsolved: had Eileen McEvoy been involved in her sister-in-law's death? It was a death knell. Mrs. McEvoy would be forced to withdraw from the activities that she loved. She would find herself "dead" to Macon's social circles, left off the invitation lists. Even if they tried to keep her on, the whispers would be too much for her to endure. Eileen was right. The damage was done.

"She was a vicious woman. She should have been shot years ago, the way she treated Juliet."

"You shouldn't be saying things like that about anyone," Monique warned.

"I don't care. It's the truth. When she married Shelby, she banished Juliet from the nursery to another floor. Then when Juliet didn't do what she wanted, she'd lock her in her room so she couldn't get out. Kept her prisoner until she gave in and obeyed, even when she was in high school. You don't rear children like that. You don't treat anyone with that little respect.

"You'd think," Eileen went on, "someone who was into women's rights as much as Mary was back then would have been more sensitive. She was the type of person who always thought she knew what was best for everyone else, shoving her beliefs down everyone else's throat."

"I didn't know that was going on—with Juliet, I mean," Monique said.

"Of course you didn't. You were only a child yourself. Dirty little secrets. In the Sixties, no one talked about them. Now everyone goes on national TV and tells the most intimate details that I wouldn't have dared utter to my husband in the privacy of our own bedroom."

Eileen offered a mirthless smile. "It's ironic, don't you think? Shelby married Mary so that Juliet would have a mother. At least she never physically harmed the child. If she had, I would have had to step in, regardless of the scandal."

"So that's why Juliet was so unhappy," Jennifer suggested.

"No. Juliet was not unhappy," Eileen assured her. "She was getting out. She'd started college and she'd found a young man, however questionable, to love."

Malcolm Reed.

"Then why did she . . ."

Mrs. McEvoy shook her head. "I don't know."

Monique brought over a tray with three cups of coffee, spoons, a creamer, a bowl of sugar, and a stack of napkins. She set it down in the middle of the table and then shifted a cup over to Mrs. McEvoy.

She spit out her gum in a paper napkin and took a long, hard swig.

"I thought you took cream and sugar," Monique said.

"Not today." Eileen swirled the coffee hard with a spoon.

"I hope you didn't let the police see you this angry," Monique warned her.

"I know how to conduct myself properly, young lady."

Jennifer shot a sidelong glance at Monique. She supposed, once a young lady to Eileen McEvoy, always a young lady.

"I'm not the only one who had strong feelings about Mary. Melba despised her."

"The housekeeper?" Jennifer asked. "Then why did she continue to work for her?"

"Melba was devoted to Clarisse. She stayed for Shelby's sake. And for Juliet's. She watched her, all these years. Mary could only go so far with her in the house. She made sure Mary didn't cross the line with Juliet and that Shelby got the care he needed. He was sick with heart disease for two years before he died."

Eileen took another large gulp of coffee. "Mary was afraid of me, you know. She knew I'd find her weak spot now that Shelby is gone, now that I don't care who I upset. She knew I'd get her, and, if I'd had enough time, if she hadn't been killed, I would have."

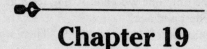

# Chapter 19

Jennifer was tired to the bone and, despite Sam's best efforts, she'd had nothing for breakfast. But shock could keep her appetite at bay for only so long.

If she were lucky, she still had enough bread and Colby cheese to make herself a grilled cheese sandwich because she sure wasn't going out for anything, and cold cereal for lunch had lost all its appeal.

Her little Beetle chugged into the parking lot of her apartment building and pulled into an open space right next to a white Chevy van with "The Art of Good Food" painted in red cursive lettering across the back and the sides. What was Arthur doing there? Her neighbors were in the same tax bracket she was. It didn't include catering costs.

She gathered her purse, slipped out of her car, and made her way up the stairs, into the building and to the elevator. At the door to her apartment, she paused. A distinct odor of garlic and onion was in the air and she could hear a low murmur coming from inside, some rap tune. Hesitantly, she raised her hand and knocked.

The door opened and Arthur, a dish towel slung over one shoulder, greeted her with a smile. "I was beginning to think you weren't going to make it home for lunch." Muffy's tail was awag as she circled Arthur, her new best friend.

"What the heck are you doing?" she demanded. Her home was her haven, inviolate. How dare he invade it and make up to her dog?

"Preparing your lunch," Arthur offered, totally ignoring her irritation. "I have a mushroom frittata about to come out of the oven."

That would explain the onion and garlic. Her gaze flicked from Arthur's grin to Muffy's panting approval to what little she could see of her kitchen. Surely if Arthur meant her harm, he wouldn't have made her lunch first. Or would he? She really was hungry. Maybe it wouldn't hurt to have one small piece of frittata before she kicked him out.

"How'd you get in here?" she demanded, dropping her bag by the door and snapping her fingers at Muffy. She trotted over for a rub behind her ears.

"Your super let me in. I told him you ordered lunch."

"I don't believe you. He knows better."

"Right. Actually I lied. I told him I was doing some fancy desserts for Dee Dee, and I needed to drop them off. He insisted on seeing my driver's license and he took down my tag numbers. For a moment there, I thought he was going to fingerprint me."

But he'd still opened the door. She'd have to have a talk with Luis. *Never* meant no exceptions, no judgment calls.

"Hey, if my being here makes you nervous, leave the door open," he told her. "I was worried about you. You had a rough night." He gave her a long, piercing look. "Why you so suspicious, girl? Can't someone look in on you without you gettin' all defensive about it?"

"I'm all right," she insisted, the door ajar.

"Well, I'm not, and when I'm not, I cook. And right now it looks as though I'm without a kitchen." He grinned at her.

"So you borrowed mine?" She wanted to add *Don't you have any friends?* but she realized it might just be that he didn't.

"Not too many people cared for Mrs. Ashton," he told her. "And it's not like I have anyone I can talk to."

"You were attached to her," Jennifer said, realizing suddenly how it made some weird sense that Arthur might choose her if he felt the need to talk. Melba was hardly the warm and cuddly type, and Eileen had made it clear how much Melba disliked Mary.

"She was good to me."

Whatever his emotions, he kept them well under control.

"And what does her death mean to your plans for your restaurant?"

He shook his head. "I don't know."

"Surely that contract you signed with her—"

"It terminated with the death of either of the parties," he said. "I dug it out of my files this morning and took another look at it."

"Did she make provisions in her will?" Jennifer asked.

Arthur shrugged. "I haven't heard nothin' 'bout the will yet. I'm hopin' for a call from her lawyer, but that all takes time. As of right now, I'm unemployed and the Art of Good Food is on hiatus until I find me another kitchen. Melba won't let me in the door. I've made her a list of my equipment, but she says I can't remove anything until it's okayed by the executor, and I don't even know who that is at the moment. She suggested I make copies of all my receipts."

"I see. Who made her the guard?"

"The police told her to lock it up until Mrs. A's lawyer takes care of things. I've had to cancel a number of jobs. Tell you what, I'll just refer them to Dee Dee."

"Thanks. She could use the work. Hey, maybe she could arrange some kind of cooperative venture. You could share her kitchen, at least for a little while. I could ask her, real subtle like."

He offered that engaging grin of his. " 'Fraid I've got too much going on right now, too many arrangements to make."

Jennifer nodded. His life had been turned upside down.

The timer beeped in the kitchen.

"Excuse me. Your lunch is ready." Arthur disappeared behind the partition. She didn't bother to follow him. She simply pulled out a chair at the table, sat down, and let Muffy welcome her home.

In less than two minutes, Arthur returned carrying two bowls of greens. "Hope you like Caesar salad," he told her, placing one on the place mat in front of her. A basket of fresh rolls was already on the table. "The frittata needs to stand a few minutes before I cut it. Got some of the prettiest cantaloupe from the farmer's market sliced and ready to go."

"Sounds wonderful. Arthur," she started, looking up at him, "why would someone want Mary Ashton dead?"

He slid into a chair across from her and leaned forward, his elbows on the table. "Mrs. A's an acquired taste, but I don't know anyone, 'ceptin' maybe Mrs. McEvoy, who actually hated her. What you've got to remember is she had money. Lots of money and that house has to be worth a fortune. What I wonder is who couldn't wait? Who had to have it now? And how could killing her let them get it? I'd say the answer is pretty obvious." He took a bite of salad and then hopped back up. "Forgot the tea."

He was back in seconds. He must have had the drinks sitting on the counter. He handed her one and she took a sip. Perfectly brewed with just a hint of mint. Distinctive. He evidently liked to leave his mark on everything he did.

"Why do you think it's obvious who killed her?"

"Mrs. A wasn't into anything illegal, she wasn't cheatin' on anyone or tryin' to steal some other woman's man. It has to be the house, and I only know one person who could lay claim to it, will or no."

"You mean Mrs. McEvoy."

He nodded and handed her the bread basket.

She plucked out a round, nicely browned yeast roll, so light she had to be careful not to crush it.

"Did Mrs. Ashton tell you about the threats?"

"What threats?" he asked, slathering his roll with butter.

"She entrusted me with threats that had been left for her in the house."

"You kiddin' me? So that's why she had you there. I knew somethin' must be up. She didn't have any stay-over company since I started working for her."

"Yep. She said Mrs. McEvoy wrote them."

"See? What'd I tell you? I suppose you turned them over to the police."

She nodded. "Just like Mrs. Ashton asked me to."

"Good." Arthur grinned at her. She studied his face, trying not to be too obvious about it.

"So, what's on your schedule now?" Arthur asked.

"I don't know."

"What you mean you don't know? You got a whole life to pick back up. Nobody puttin' locks on your doors."

"Mrs. Ashton didn't want her murderer to get away with it."

"And you made sure she won't. You delivered the

threats and told the police what you know. Your part's done with."

"I know, it's just—"

"Just nothin'. She paid you, you did all that she asked, now forget it."

"But what if it wasn't Eileen, Arthur? What if Mary was mistaken?"

"What kind of wild idea you got in your head now?"

"I don't know, but I understand Melba hated her, too. She had free run of that house. She got in my room to let Muffy out with no problem."

"Now there you go gettin' sidetracked. I'm sure Mrs. Ashton knew better than anyone who wanted her dead. Wouldn't you? Besides, what would Melba have to gain now?"

"What did she have to gain before?" Jennifer asked, suddenly aware of the implication.

"Look, I don't like to talk out of school. He's dead now anyway."

"You're talking about Shelby, aren't you? Is that why Melba stayed on? Was there something going on between the two of them?" It was strange for her to think of older people like that, maybe being in love, or at least one in love with the other, and never settling it between the two of them.

"Nah. Heck, I don't know anything about it. All's I know once he became ill, she took care of him like he was her own baby, waitin' on him, shushin' the rest of us, even Mary, like we had no right to be around him. But none of this is no matter. You think too much. You need to let it all go."

"Good advice."

"That's right. Now get on with your salad. I didn't come all the way over here and cook just to have you sit and stare at my food."

She broke off a piece of bread. It melted in her mouth. But something kept nagging in the back of her mind even as he got up to bring in the frittata. Something didn't seem quite right, if only she could figure out what it was.

# Chapter 20

Melba would know. Jennifer was convinced of it as she guided her car mindlessly up Vineville Avenue on the excuse that getting out of her apartment, even for a few minutes, might help to clear her head. Jennifer flicked off the radio. As much as she liked Santana, she needed quiet.

Melba would know who, other than Eileen, might have been a threat to Mary, and how that person could have delivered those notes, assuming she hadn't done it herself.

Melba's planting them would be the simplest solution, but, if she'd murdered Mary, why had she gone to such lengths when a little something extra in the afternoon tea would have been a whole lot easier and probably never questioned?

Hatred. Brutal, raw hatred. It drove some people to take chances they otherwise would never take. But had Melba hated Mary that much? If she did, how could she have stayed in that house all these years, especially after Shelby died?

But the biggest question of all, at least for the moment, was how to get Melba to talk to her.

She found her Beetle moving on autopilot toward the historic district. What could it hurt, just to swing by the house for a quick look? She drove past, parked two streets over at one of the municipal parks, and walked back along the shaded sidewalks to the Ashton mansion. She hoped she didn't look half as conspicuous as she felt.

Maybe she could scout around the building, get some idea of how many outside doors there were and where they lay, while she figured out a scheme to approach Melba. How those threats were delivered could hold the key to Mary's murder.

The police seemed to be gone, at least for now, but crime-scene tape was stretched between the columns to block the front door. Another tape ran all the way around the front yard from the brick wall on one side to the tall hedge on the other. She looked both ways, then slipped under the tape and circled around the driveway toward the back of the house. She wasn't about to touch anything, only look. What could that hurt? There had to be an entrance leading up from the basement and one in the rear of the house, and, quite possibly, one on one side. Or maybe not. Security had to have been a consideration.

Years of vegetation hugged the stone foundation, mostly flowering shrubs—azaleas and rhododendrons—with annuals—impatiens and johnny-jump-ups—forming a narrow border between them and the grass. It didn't look as though a person could slip behind the thick growth even if there were a window that could easily be jimmied. They certainly couldn't do it without leaving evidence that they'd squeezed through. But, as best as she could see, nothing had been disturbed.

When she arrived at the back of the house, she froze. The doors to one of the outbuildings stood open. Someone was on the property.

She heard a metallic screech across stone and saw Melba emerging from behind a tall hedge, struggling with a wrought-iron patio chair.

"Need some help with that?" Jennifer offered, her heart rate returning almost to normal.

Melba, dressed in overalls and with a scarf around her hair, looked up, startled, but she recovered quickly. She wiped her brow with the back of her arm and then pulled a cell phone out of her pocket and brandished it. "You're trespassing. I'll give you thirty seconds to get out of here. Then I'm calling 911."

"Will you? I suspect you're not supposed to be here, either. I didn't see your name listed as an exception on that 'do not cross' tape, and I don't think the police will look kindly on someone tampering with a murder scene."

"I can't leave this furniture outside. Somebody will steal it. Everybody who can read half a sentence or has turned on a TV or radio in the last twenty-four hours knows this house is empty. What do you expect me to do?" She slipped the phone back into her pocket.

"Whatever you like. But I need to talk to you."

The woman's eyes narrowed. "Me? Mary allowed you under her roof for one night, and she wound up dead. I don't have anything to say to the likes of you."

"You really believe I let someone in the house, don't you?"

"If you didn't, who did?"

Jennifer shrugged. "If I had to bet, I'd say you know this house better than anybody living."

From the stony look on her face, Jennifer realized Melba was not about to have Jennifer turn the tables on her. "What business could that ever be of yours?"

"Mary made it my business."

"So it's Mary now, is it? You meet her on Sunday, move in on Monday, and by Tuesday, when she's dead, you're on a first-name basis with her."

"You have keys to the house," Jennifer pointed out. "And you know the security system."

"And I live alone and saw no one after I went home for the night. You won't cast your suspicions in my direction."

"How much privacy did you afford the Ashtons over the years? How many secrets were you privy to?" Jennifer knew she shouldn't have said it, even as the words were tumbling out.

Melba seethed. Without a retort, she drew the phone from her pocket and pushed in three numbers. "I want to report a prowler. . . ."

Jennifer didn't wait to hear the rest of her sentence. Melba was not one to cut anyone any slack, and once she disliked someone, Jennifer suspected that she didn't change her mind.

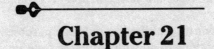

# Chapter 21

If Jennifer had been tired earlier, she wasn't quite sure what to call what she was experiencing now, maybe a total body meltdown.

The answering machine light was blinking frantically when she opened her door.

Beeeeep!

*Jennifer, where have you been? I've been calling all afternoon.* Dee Dee sounded anxious. *Five people have called me since two o'clock asking me for our services starting this Friday night and on into the next three weeks. I already had that child's party and an anniversary dinner scheduled for Sunday. These are big clients, Jen, and I don't want to give them up. I can handle a couple of these by myself and I've called Trudy and asked her to help, but some of the clients specifically—*

Beeeeep!

*I hate these machines. They never give you enough time to say what you need to. Anyway, I'll need at least three of your new vegetable bouquets and two of the rings. I tried to talk them out of it but they insisted. I know they're time consuming to make, you're busy and probably don't want to do it, especially with this late—*

Beeeeep!

*Lots of cursing going on over here. Just glad I've got*

105

*you on speed dial. See what you can do. And, oh, they want your broccoli salad, too. Call me.*

Beeeeep!

*Me, again. You're the best, Jen. Sorry if I sound like a shrew.*

At the moment, Jennifer had only one purpose in life, and it had nothing to do with writing or catering. It had to do with sleep. She grabbed the cord to the machine and yanked it out of the wall.

In a galaxy far, far away the phone was ringing. Or so she wished. She'd like to send that phone into space.

Jennifer fumbled for the receiver on her bedside table, stretched too far, and went tumbling out of bed, tangling in her sheet and taking her alarm clock down with her. She lay flat on her back, like a butterfly stuck in a cocoon, staring at the ceiling, listening to the phone ring and wondering why she felt such compulsion to answer the blasted thing when four out of five times it was a telemarketer. She actually owned a working answering machine. Why the heck wasn't it picking up? Then she remembered that she'd unplugged it.

Muffy trotted around from the other side of the bed, stared down at her, panting, her tail wagging vigorously, then leaned down and slurped at her cheek.

She pushed Muffy away, and the creature slunk back. Darn. She didn't mean to hurt her feelings, but it was far too early to deal with dog germs. She rubbed at her cheek as she tried to rise up, but the sheet had her firmly anchored.

Rinnnnng!

"That's all right, sweetie," Jennifer assured the dog, reaching out a hand. But Muffy knew when she'd been rejected. She pulled back, just out of petting distance, and purposely ignored her.

Rinnnnng!

She picked up the alarm clock off the floor where it had landed beside her. It read ten thirty. The rays of light escaping into the room through her closed miniblinds assured her it was A.M., not P.M. She hadn't slept through the entire day after all. Another goal shot all to heck.

And again the phone rang. She pushed herself up and stretched far enough to strain the muscle in her back and grab the receiver, the body of the phone toppling off the table, just missing her head. She offered a hoarse hello.

"I was getting worried about you. You sound terrible. Is everything all right?"

"Leigh Ann, I was asleep."

"Really? I'm sorry. Should I call back later?"

Jennifer groaned. "What is it?"

"I only have a minute. My boss finally stepped out of the office. I'm just reporting in. Don't operatives report in?"

That's right. She'd put Leigh Ann on assignment. She tried to get her eyes to open wider, but they weren't cooperating. "So what did you find out?"

"I finally got that Douglas Wexler on the phone yesterday afternoon, but he refused to talk to me. He said everything he knows is in his book, and he doesn't vouch for any of it. Says he just reports what he's told, doesn't confirm or deny the existence of ghosts. He refused to give me the name of his source for Amy Loggins and then had the nerve to try to sell me his new book, a two-volume set about the ghosts of Atlanta."

"I see. So when do you get it?"

"No later than Tuesday. It's coming express."

"Remind me again why you woke me up?" Jennifer's phone made one of those annoying beeps that signals that another call is coming in. "Hold on just a moment, Leigh Ann." She pushed the flash button. "Hello."

"What do you mean going off to stay in some woman's house and not telling anyone where you were going?" It was Teri.

Not telling anyone obviously meant not telling *her*.

"You are all right, aren't you?" Teri added.

"Yes." If being trapped in her own bedroom like a mummy was all right.

"Did Leigh Ann tell you what we found out?"

"She was just about to when you beeped in. She's on the other line."

"Don't move a muscle." As if she could. "I'll beep in with Leigh Ann and get us all on conference call."

Modern technology. Thank goodness none of them yet owned a video phone.

"You still there?" Leigh Ann asked.

"Unfortunately, yes," Jennifer told them.

"We found out one thing," Leigh Ann said. "Rich people don't like to answer their doors. And the ones who do sure don't like to talk about ghosts." Leigh Ann sighed.

"Does that mean you two had no luck?" Jennifer asked.

"Heck, no," Teri said. "You give us an assignment and we don't come back until we've got it."

"Then you found the person this Wexler talked to about the Loggins sightings."

"I think so, or someone just as good," Leigh Ann assured her. "A lane runs behind the Ashton mansion. There's not a huge amount of land with those houses. They were in-town houses, after all. A lot of the people who built them had plantations in the country. We scouted around the house to a point where we could get a good view of those two windows in the back, on the corner of the third floor. We figured—"

"Excuse me," Teri interrupted.

"That is, Teri figured that someone seeing anything in that room had to live on that back lane, and as they wouldn't talk to us at their doors—"

"Leigh Ann pretended to be conducting a survey. She'd ring the bell, pull out a notebook, and start in with 'We're recording psychic phenomena in the area.' "

"So anyway Teri had this idea that we might catch someone out on the lane going for a walk, and we did."

"Some old codger with a slow, shuffling gait, and a dog the size of his fist on a twelve-foot leash."

"Oh, it couldn't have been that long," Leigh Ann insisted.

"Do you mind?" Jennifer asked. If she didn't love them, she would have hung up and let them talk to each other. No telling how long it'd take for them to notice.

"We tried to make friends with his dog. Meanest little critter. Bit the blood out of my finger. Anyway, Teri started talking about how it creeped her out to be in that neighborhood at night after what happened to Mary. Very smooth. Then I threw in the part about Amy Loggins's ghost."

"That man had the slowest drawl I've ever heard," Teri added. "I mean he just could not get those words out. It was painful. By the time he got to the end of the sentence you'd forget what the first part was about."

"What did he say?" Jennifer asked.

"He heard something the night Mary died," Leigh Ann said. "He lives in the house just behind the Ashtons. It woke him up. He described it as a soft, low moan of her name, 'Mary, Mary,' being carried by the breeze real eerielike. He only heard it twice, but he was sure it was the ghost calling to her dead spirit."

"Leigh Ann, that was me, screaming out the window at the top of my lungs," Jennifer told her.

"Oh," Leigh Ann said.

"How old was this guy?" Jennifer added.

"I don't know. What would you say, Teri?"

"Really old. He said he remembered Amy Loggins when she was alive, so he has to be ancient."

"He told us he used to watch her," Leigh Ann added, "up there in that room, her hair wild, her eyes even wilder, pressing her face up against the glass, looking out as far as she could see from her room, watching for Sherman, watching for the burnings," Leigh Ann said. "Of course she was an old woman by then."

"He said his father told him she got out once," Teri added. "Scared the bejesus out of the whole neighborhood. They sent a search party out for her."

"How'd she manage it?" Jennifer asked, rolling over and tugging part way out of the sheet. "Melba told me they kept her bolted in."

"He didn't say. I don't think he knew. They finally found her almost two days later hiding in a wooded area about a mile away. Dehydrated and crazier than ever."

"Did he know about the two sightings in the ghost book?"

"Yep, but he wouldn't say who spoke to Wexler, only that they were true. And that it had happened again. That the night Mary died, for the first time in years, he saw a light shining in Amy's room and the shadow of someone moving about in it when he took his dog out for his final walk."

"Of course he did," Jennifer agreed. "That was me again."

"I knew that," Teri said.

"Of course you did," Jennifer agreed. "Listen up gals. I want you both at my house tonight, at seven o'clock. Can you make it?"

"Yeah, but why? You're not doing that rounding up of the usual suspects thing, are you?"

"Not unless you've suddenly become a suspect," Jennifer assured her. "Just be here. Call the others for me please, and don't be late. I've got to get some rest tonight, one way or the other."

She dropped the phone back into its cradle. She really needed to get up. She had more people to talk to, and the one who came most readily to mind was Luther Johnson, Arthur's grandfather. He'd been around so long, he had to know something. Yes, she had to talk to him, providing she could force herself up off the floor.

Muffy, who couldn't hold a grudge, came over and snuggled up against her. Jennifer's hand found the soft fur of the dog's neck as she rolled over on her back. It'd been a long time since Jennifer had slept on the floor.

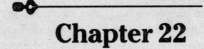

# Chapter 22

"I'm older than dirt," Luther Johnson told Jennifer, thunking his cane into the worn carpet. "A person shouldn't let himself get so old and useless. It ain't right. What you say you come here for again? I know it wasn't just to hear me complain."

Jennifer smiled at him. She felt certain he didn't mean half of what he was saying to her. He was teasing her. He had a glint in the corner of his dark eye and a slight curve to his mouth. His white beard and mustache were too well groomed for a man who had given up on life, and the house was perfectly kept, not a speck of dust in sight.

"Arthur told me you worked for the Ashtons for years." Jennifer tried to settle back into the slipcovered chair, but it threatened to swallow her whole. She pushed herself forward.

"That's right. Hired on shortly after Mr. Shelby's second marriage."

"You've heard about Mrs. Ashton's murder?"

"I said I was old, young lady, not deaf, dumb, and blind. Or dead. What kind of a hole do you think I live in?" He adjusted the glasses that had slipped to the end of his nose and gave her a quick once over. "I've got myself cable TV, and I can still see well enough to read the newspaper."

Jennifer blushed, feeling thoroughly put in her place. "I was in the house the night she died, and. . . ."

"And you're feeling guilty." He nodded his head and took up a pipe, busily stuffing it with tobacco. Then he leaned forward and fussed through a stack of newspapers on the table next to his recliner. "Where is that dang lighter?"

Jennifer retrieved it from under the edge of a magazine on the coffee table and handed it to him. He seemed a little too agitated. "You understand about the guilt."

He flicked on the lighter and sucked the fire down into the bowl of tobacco, watching her over the pipe, but he didn't say a word. He just let the smoke puff out of his mouth around the stem.

"Arthur told me about your finding Juliet," she told him.

"That Arthur talks more than he should."

"Maybe. I spent the night in Juliet's room. It made me want to know why—"

"Some people, no matter how hard you try, can't be saved," he said more to himself than to her. "That's a life lesson, young 'un. You'd do well to learn it now."

"What did she need saving from?"

"People make choices and gosh darn if they don't act all surprised by the consequences. Does that make any sense to you?"

"What choice did Juliet make?"

"How much pit bull you got in your lineage? You're as directed as my old hound Sal. She'd tree a fox and sit there as long as it took to get him down."

"I'll take that as a compliment, if you'll let me."

He grinned. "I did love that old dog, but why you diggin' what happened to Juliet back up now? Can't do you or nobody else no good. Times have changed. The world moved on, at least all save maybe Mr. Shelby. God, but what he loved that child." His eyes filled.

Obviously Shelby wasn't the only one who had loved Juliet.

"Shame's a powerful motivator," he went on. "We used to have too much of it. Now we don't have enough. You think there might have been sometime in between when we got it just right?"

"I doubt it. What was Juliet ashamed of?"

"Did I say anything about Juliet being ashamed?" His eyes narrowed.

"No, but I thought you meant—"

"Sometimes people think too much. You one of those people?"

"Most definitely."

That made him laugh, a snicker that turned into a belly laugh. "I think I like you. You and old Sal would have made quite a pair. You say that was you they wrote about in the paper who was there the night Miss Mary died?"

"That was me."

"Hmmm, hmmmm, hmmmmm. You don't have no better sense than to stay in a place like that."

"You worked there."

"But I didn't *stay* there. Only the once."

"When?"

"Miss Mary had Mr. Shelby's body laid out in the parlor for the viewing."

"In the house?"

"Tradition. His daddy's body had been there and his daddy's before him."

"And you stayed with it?"

"Somebody has to sit up with the dead. Wouldn't be right to leave them alone."

Little shivers pricked up her arms, even in the heat of that small clapboard house.

"But you weren't even working there then."

"Wasn't work I was doing. Mr. Shelby and me go way back."

"Weren't you . . ." The words had escaped her mouth before she could stop them.

"Scared?" He chuckled at her. "Lots more than spirits to be scared of, child. Spirits, they come to you, chat a while, and move on. They don't mean no harm to the living. It's people you should be afraid of, if'n you've a mind to be afraid."

"It's just that I didn't know anybody still did that."

"Most don't, but that's what Mr. Shelby asked for, just like he done for his daughter."

"Juliet? She was laid out in the house?"

He nodded and puffed slowly on his pipe. "She was the last one before Mr. Shelby. Like I said, he was strong on tradition."

"And did you . . ."

"Sit up with her?" He shook his head. "Mr. Shelby never left her side, not to eat or to drink. I brought him food and tea, but he wouldn't touch it, wouldn't even acknowledge my presence."

The loss of a child. What grief to bear.

"Did Mary . . . did she wait up too?"

"Mr. Shelby wouldn't allow it. He wanted no one in there. Not me, not Melba, not even Miss Mary."

"Actually . . ."

"You meant for Mr. Shelby?"

Jennifer nodded.

"Melba and I took care of it, but it was mostly me."

"Why?"

"Melba took Mr. Shelby's death real hard. She did what had to be done, making the funeral arrangements, preparing for the viewing, and the reception following the internment, but that night, when no one much was around, I heard her sobbing. I sent her off to bed. No need her exhausting herself further. She didn't need to be up talking to him like that all night. If she'd had anything important to say, she should have said it while he was alive. You don't do that, Missy, do ya? You got somethin' to say, you tell it to a person while they're living. You can't be sure how much they hear after they're dead. No need making amends then."

"What kind of amends?"

"Now that would be between the three of them."

"Three?"

"Melba, Mr. Shelby, and God. Ain't none of my business."

The whole idea of waiting up with the dead fascinated her, almost as much as it repulsed her. "And when Clarisse died and Amy Loggins died . . ."

"I 'spect they was both done the same way, but I wouldn't know."

No wonder the house had such a feel to it, especially the parlor.

"You worked in that house a long time. Tell me, who hated Mrs. Ashton enough to murder her?"

"Now you're asking me to see into the hearts of men. I don't rightly know who might have done somethin' to her. Didn't seem to me nobody much cared one way or t'other if she lived or died. That happens to some of us when we get older. You got to plant your good deeds early, so they have time to blossom in your old age."

The wood on the screen door rattled with what Jennifer assumed was supposed to be a knock.

"Come in," Luther shouted.

A lively middle-aged woman with a bright dimpled face and a Styrofoam container let herself in. Her face went slack when she saw Jennifer, but she recovered quickly. "Oh, I'm sorry, Luther. I didn't realize you had company," she said, handing him the container. It emitted an aroma of tomato sauce and peaches.

"What you got for me today, Gert?"

"Spaghetti and meatballs with salad and fresh cobbler."

"Gosh darn it! Didn't you tell them that I said spaghetti doesn't travel well?"

"The message was delivered. Aren't any of our people professional chefs like you," the woman reminded him.

"They get paid, don't they?"

"Yes, I suppose they do."

"That makes them professional. They should know their business. Doesn't take a whole lot more to do a job well than to just do it."

"Do you want it now or should I put it in the fridge?"

"You can throw the danged thing out the window for all I care," Luther fussed.

Gert winked at Jennifer. "That means put it in the fridge." She disappeared for a moment, then swished back through, paused at the door, and waved. "See you tomorrow, Luther."

"She's a right nice lady even if she doesn't listen worth a hoot."

"I can tell," Jennifer agreed. "Eileen McEvoy seems like a nice lady, too."

"She can be."

"I'm sure you're aware the police suspect her in Mary Ashton's death."

He nodded.

"Well, what do you think? Could she have done it?"

He chuckled at her. "Miss Eileen is a lady. No matter how much she despised Miss Mary, she'd leave her to God to deal with. That's her belief and I can't see her breaking it."

But sometimes people were a little too anxious to wait for God's justice. "You didn't finish telling me about Melba and Shelby. What regrets did she have to make right with him?"

"It wasn't her fault, what happened to Juliet. Wasn't mine either. But sometimes you suspect somethin' and you don't move quick like. Later you wish you'd trusted your instincts. A person shouldn't force her beliefs on nobody else. We come to know what we can bear in our own way. Can't nobody else tell you what your conscience can take and what it can't."

"What are you saying? Did Juliet feel guilty about something?"

Luther's face turned hard. "I'm not saying nothin', just an old man ramblin' on."

He picked up the remote control and turned on CNN. Their interview was over.

# Chapter 23

"Eileen hated her, and I don't mean just a little," Jennifer told Sam, standing over him and tapping her finger nervously on the edge of his office desk. "I mean we're talking deep-rooted, I'm-gonna-get-you-sucker hate. Anyone who saw her at Monique's could tell you that. And Arthur said it, too. Only, both Luther and Monique said they couldn't see Eileen hurting anyone, too religious. And Melba—well, who knows what that woman is thinking? But there was no love lost for Mary there, either."

She'd had to wait ten minutes for Sam to get back to the office when she got there just after three, and every thought she had in her head was anxiously bubbling out.

Actually she was lucky he'd come back at all. When he was out that late on assignment, sometimes he didn't return. He simply finished up at home and e-mailed his copy.

"You should be home sleeping," he reminded her, "instead of collecting character references for Eileen McEvoy."

"I know. I did sleep most of the morning." She didn't bother to tell him that half of it was on the floor. "But I'm fully alert now." She blinked her eyes wide at him.

"So I see. Your mind has slipped into overdrive."

"Actually it's more like mush, but active mush."

"And this mush has concluded what? That you think Eileen had Mary killed?" Sam leaned forward and pulled a yellow legal pad from a pile of papers on his right, his pen poised over it. "Sometimes people can convince themselves that if they don't actually have a hand in the deed, they're somehow not as responsible as the person they hired to commit the crime."

She sat down on top of his desk and took the pad away from him. "Heck if I know if she's guilty or not. I couldn't help but like the woman. She's full of righteous indignation, not blood lust. I can see her committing social murder without blinking an eye; that is, putting Mary through public humiliation so bad her phone would never ring again, like some avenging angel pointing her finger at evil. Only she wouldn't do that when Shelby or Juliet was alive. She realized it would hurt them as well."

"Maybe the point is they're both dead," Sam offered. "The courts let her down. You say Mary had pretty much withdrawn from most of her social engagements. Maybe her life was all she had left."

"What a grim thought." She shook her head. "Like I said, Luther seemed to think that Eileen would leave Mary to God's judgment, but I don't know."

"Sometimes even religious people can convince themselves that taking the law into their own hands is somehow doing God's work. Who is Luther, by the way?"

"*Was*, actually. The Ashtons' cook up until three years ago. But *is*, too, as he's still alive."

"I see. I'm glad to hear you're restricting your communications to the living."

She let that one go. She had no intentions of allowing Sam to sidetrack her. "But you should have heard Eileen talking about Juliet. She knew that child was being mistreated. She just didn't feel there was anything she could do about it. How frustrating! Shelby was there in the

Home. It was his responsibility. Eileen was only the aunt. And Luther and Melba—they carry the guilt, too."

"You're talking about events that happened years ago. You shouldn't let yourself get worked up over something that's long over and done. You need to answer a simple question for yourself: in your gut, do you believe Eileen McEvoy is behind the killing of Mary Ashton?"

"Haven't you been listening to me?"

Sam let out an exasperated puff of air. "That's exactly my problem. I have."

"Okay, then. No, I don't. I can't see Eileen doing the blood-and-guts thing, not now, not then. Not ever, actually, especially now when all that's left to be concerned about is property. Under all that outward gentility, Southern women are as strong and determined as they come. But they're hardly ever obvious."

Sam raised an eyebrow. "I certainly agree with that."

Jennifer grimaced at him. He was really good at simultaneously complimenting and insulting her, especially when she set herself up.

"Mrs. McEvoy told me that Shelby married Mary so he'd have someone to take care of Juliet," she said. "Mary told me that she was the love of Shelby's life, but Monique disagrees. Throw in Mrs. McEvoy's description of how Mary treated Juliet, and Shelby's loss of interest in life after Juliet's death. And let's not forget Mary's reaction, at least according to Luther, after Shelby died: she didn't sit up with his body."

"I didn't know people still did that."

"Some do, apparently. But my point is that somebody's not got the whole picture."

"Yeah, us."

"And then there's Melba. According to Mrs. McEvoy, she *really* didn't like Mary. Yet she stayed in that house all these years and Arthur—"

"I'm beginning to think I need a playbill. Who's Arthur?"

"The current cook, Luther's grandson. He implied that Melba might have had a thing for Shelby, and Luther told me she cried all night when he died."

"I see. Sounds like a hotbed of romantic intrigue."

"Actually, I think it was anything but."

"I found out something you might find of interest," Sam offered. "Some items were missing from her room."

"Mrs. Ashton's? Are you serious?"

"Mostly jewelry. Small items. Expensive pieces."

"That wasn't a robbery," Jennifer insisted. "If you had seen that room, you'd know that." She didn't notice she was trembling until Sam took her hand.

"Why are you pursuing this?" he asked. "It's not good for you. I want to get a story, but what interest do you have in it other than curiosity?"

She pulled her hand away, not expecting him to understand what she was about to say. "Monique asked me to. And I took Mary Ashton's money, all one thousand dollars of it, and now I don't have anybody to give it back to even if I wanted to."

"So? She's dead. That negates any contract you may have had with her. Besides, she said you could keep the money."

"It's not just the money. She made me promise."

"Promise what?"

"That I wouldn't let whoever murdered her get away with it. Sam, she thought she was going to die, but not like that. You didn't hear the terror in her screams. Even if she were everything that Mrs. McEvoy said, she didn't deserve that. No one does. Juliet had somehow made it through. She had made a life for herself."

"Then why did she commit suicide?"

Jennifer shook her head. "I don't know."

Sam studied her. "Mrs. Ashton's reading glasses were gone, too."

"Maybe she was wearing them when they attacked her. She could have been reading before bed, maybe even fallen asleep with them on. Her attackers took away everything they could, everything except the blood. They couldn't take that away."

"Okay. What do you want me to do?"

"I want you to get access for me to the back files of the *Telegraph*. There had to be a write-up about the wedding at least, maybe an engagement announcement, a mention of the honeymoon. I'd like to know exactly what was going on between those two and how Mary managed to sweep Shelby out from under Melba's feet when Clarisse died. I'd like to know how Shelby came to hire Mary, where she came from, anything to help me understand the animosity between Mary and Eileen. I can't help but feel the answers lie somehow in Mary's character. It couldn't have all been about Juliet. And Juliet's death, too—there'd be some mention of it in the newspaper, wouldn't there? Even if her father tried to hush it up?"

"Of course, although I can't see how what happened way back then has to do with Mary's murder."

"The hatred that caused that slaughter had to be long-standing. Mary hasn't been active enough in the last few years to rile anyone to that kind of anger, at least not as best I can tell. If we're lucky, some conflict might have been hinted at in the newspaper. Besides, the police have the house wrapped up tight with crime tape."

"Don't tell me you were considering—"

"Would I do something illegal?"

"Nothing above a fourth- or fifth-degree misdemeanor, but that can get you into trouble, too."

"So, can you get me into the files?"

He paused, seeming to consider her request. "I'll call Ned and let him know we're coming down to the morgue."

He knew her well enough to realize she had to keep busy when something like this upset her. She'd go wherever her instincts led her. His job was to either help or step out of the way.

He stood up, tightened his tie, and slipped on his sport coat.

"You're coming with me?"

"Sure. Are you kidding? You may just find some angle I can use in an article. I don't suppose you'd agree to let me in on it if I didn't come."

"Not a chance."

"That's what I thought. This promises, assuming it's ever solved, to be quite a story. One of Macon's richest women is murdered in a historic mansion—"

"A haunted historic mansion," Jennifer added.

He grinned at her. "Right. It doesn't get much better than that."

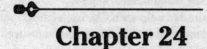

# Chapter 24

"You'd think there'd be an easier way to find information," Jennifer groaned.

"Someday, when it's all on computer, there will be," Sam assured her. "But for now it's pick a date, find the microfiche, and rummage."

"I wish I knew exactly when Juliet died, but it must have been sometime in October of seventy-two." She zipped through a week's worth of film.

"If you're looking just for the obits, they won't have much in them. Look for a news story."

She nodded. That was exactly what she was doing. She had her mind set to search for "Ashton" as she scanned article headlines. "Boy, abortion was a hot topic even in those days."

"Especially in those days. A year later the Supreme Court made their ruling striking down laws prohibiting abortion in both Texas and Georgia," Sam reminded her.

It was interesting stuff, and if she'd had the time, she'd like to read it. She zipped again. More abortion controversy. She was about to press the button once more when the search portion of her brain kicked in and Mary Ashton's name leapt out at her. Quickly, she read the article.

"Look at this," she told Sam. "Mary Ashton was heavily involved in the movement to make abortions legal. I know Monique mentioned that Mary was active with women's issues, but I had no idea she was actually lobbying for something like this."

"You said she was a nurse, right?"

"She was hired to help with Clarisse's care."

"All right then. She may have seen one too many botched abortions wherever she worked."

"Or maybe she just liked to be in control," Jennifer suggested. Or maybe she'd had an illegal one herself. Somehow Jennifer suspected that Mary was the type who dealt with everything on a personal level.

Sam looked at his watch. "We don't have a great deal of time. Ned's going to be kicking us out before too long. Unlike the rest of us, he likes to work regular hours."

That was her cue to hurry along.

She recognized Juliet immediately when her picture came up. It must have been from high school because she was wearing a drape, smiling, lovely, so very young, full of potential, that long dark hair parted in the middle and hanging straight down the sides of her face. The headline read "Young Socialite Commits Suicide."

She had the same reaction she'd had to every other photo she'd seen of Juliet—pity. It made her heart ache. "It says she was an honor student with plans to major in journalism."

Coincidence or Malcolm's influence?

"Friends reported she'd become despondent the week before her death," Jennifer went on. "It appeared to be a classic case of depression ending in suicide. Her father could not be reached for comment."

"Does it mention a history of mental illness?" Sam asked.

"Nope. If she was being treated, I'm sure her daddy could keep it quiet."

"Without a doubt. It's getting late. Are you about finished?"

"One more thing while we're here." She hopped up and retrieved the roll of film covering 1959 and popped it into the machine. "Back to happier times."

She zipped past several editions, then stopped and pointed at the screen. A photo of the happy couple standing in front of a rose-covered, wooden archway took up the upper half of the front page of the living section. She scooted her metal chair closer, dragging it against the concrete floor.

"Would you look at this? May 1959. The marriage of Shelby Eliot Ashton to Mary Elizabeth Bedford at the Ashton mansion was *the* social event of the year, if not the decade. Half the population of Macon was there.

"Look how handsome he was." Jennifer tapped her finger on the image of Shelby Ashton, standing tall and straight in a dark suit.

Sam's head was so close it was almost touching hers. "Who cares about him? Get a load of her."

He was right. Mary Ashton was breathtaking, even in grainy black and white, even with hair poofed into a bouffant hairdo that has never found its way back into style. Even in a calf-length, full-skirted floral dress. No white for Shelby's second marriage.

Quickly, Jennifer scanned the article. "They were married in the house, the Reverend John Sutherland of the First Methodist Church officiating. The reception was held outside in the gardens, Eileen was Mary's matron of honor, Shelby's brother Aaron served as his best man, and Juliet was the flower girl. Apparently no one from the bride's side participated in the ceremony."

Jennifer ran the page back up to the picture. "There, in the back." She pointed to the far right of the photo where a little girl could be seen in a long, light-colored dress, lace-edged gloves, a circlet of flowers in her dark curly hair, and a small woven basket in her hand. "That must be Juliet."

"She's burying her head in some woman's skirt," Sam observed.

"Hard day for a little girl, to watch her daddy remarry." Jennifer squinted closer at the screen. "I think the woman she's holding onto is her aunt, Eileen McEvoy. At least it looks like a younger version of her. Look at the expression on her face. I don't think she was too happy about the marriage even then."

Jennifer sent the machine to the next page where the article was continued. "Listen to this: 'Mary Bedford, nanny to Miss Juliet Alison Ashton.' Eileen said Mary was Clarisse's nurse. She must have stayed on after her death to help with Juliet. Do you suppose she was living in the house when they got together? That could have really irked Melba."

"One easy way to find out. I can look up the application for the marriage license over at the courthouse," Sam suggested.

"Great. Her address will tell us. Also get a place and date of birth if it's on there."

"Will do."

"I wonder how he found her, to hire her originally, I mean."

"Maybe through an agency?"

"Most likely."

Once more, she slid the microfiche back to the photo and studied it. "Does she look happy to you? He looks happy, I think, but she looks . . ."

"Enigmatic."

"Great word, that." For a moment she sat there trying to dissect that expression, whatever it was, and trying to think what it must have been like that day, so many years ago, when Mary wed her prince charming.

"By the way, I checked with my source at the Macon Police Department." Sam always called Tim Donahue his source, even though she knew perfectly well whom he meant. As a matter of honor, he'd never told her his name. "They used her toothbrush and some hairs from her hairbrush to determine her DNA. It was all hers," he whispered, leaning in close to her ear. "Every drop of blood they tested belonged to Mary Ashton."

She closed her eyes and hugged her shoulders. No matter what had happened since her wedding day, Mary must have been filled with hopes and dreams that day. "So that's how her fairy tale ended."

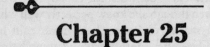

# Chapter 25

"It's called a brainstorming session, and, no, it doesn't always have to be about books," Jennifer told Teri, offering her a can of ginger ale and then sliding another across her dining table in April's direction. "I've been spending too much time speculating on motives. Now it's time to get back to the physical evidence. Didn't somebody once say something like, 'If you know how a crime was committed, you know who did it?' "

"No big mystery there," Teri said under her breath. "One very sharp object met up with one very defenseless old lady."

"I'm not just talking about what happened to Mary," Jennifer insisted. "Someone made sure I couldn't get out of that room the night Mary died." She tossed an unopened bag of dried banana chips to Leigh Ann. "I want to know who. And why. And how they got in the house in the first place."

Leigh Ann caught the bag, looked at its label, and threw it back. "You shouldn't rule out supernatural forces," she offered, her legs propped on one of the spare dining chairs. "They say ghosts get irritated when people occupy their space, and we all know how strange poltergeist phenomena can be. They actually move objects."

Teri rolled her eyes. "That's ridiculous. Poltergeists only appear in the presence of adolescents." She was sitting on the floor next to the sofa, refusing to crowd around the table. Teri liked her space. And she liked her meat. She chewed on a beef jerky stick she'd brought from home.

"Since when were you into the paranormal?" Jennifer asked.

"What?" Teri asked defensively. "I do my research. I wrote a ghost story once."

"You never shared it with us," April said.

"Lucky for you," Teri assured her. "I threw it away."

Muffy snuggled up against Teri and let out a long sigh, no doubt wishing she could have a bite of jerky, and laid her head in her lap.

"But back to the block under the door. I hardly think Amy Loggins's ghost wedged something under Jennifer's door." Teri stroked the dog's fur and cooed at her. She was better with animals than she generally was with people—especially Leigh Ann.

"You said you were on the third floor, right, actually sleeping in the room that Amy occupied?" Leigh Ann asked, ignoring Teri's comment.

Jennifer nodded, a warning look in her eyes. "But it was more recently Juliet Ashton's room." She was not about to let Leigh Ann turn the discussion into a woo-woo session.

"I can't believe you were right in the center of all the psychic emanations in that house!"

"Quit it, Leigh Ann!" Teri insisted, grabbing a small pillow off the sofa behind her and throwing it in her direction. It bounced off the chair and landed on the floor. "You're not helping."

"What?" She shrugged, a mischievous grin playing about her mouth. She truly believed in the possibility of ghosts, ESP, and the tarot, but she was no airhead. She was simply a romantic who liked to keep her options open, and she was not above teasing. But she could also be a drama queen. Sometimes it was hard to know which was which.

"Seriously," Leigh Ann said, more soberly, "for all we know, Amy was looking out for you, protecting you."

"Sort of like a guardian angel," April suggested.

"Exactly," Leigh Ann agreed. "You said the block simply vanished."

"I did not. I said it was missing," Jennifer reminded her, picking the pillow up and tossing it back at Teri. It landed on Muffy's head. She shook it off and snuggled back down against Teri.

"Okay," Leigh Ann continued. "We already know that at least one someone other than Mary and yourself was in that house that night. Someone *human*. She was killed, after all. That means, to swipe the block, the killer must have been on your floor sometime after you left your room."

Leigh Ann dropped a handful of April's chocolate-covered raisins into her mouth and proceeded to talk around them. "These aren't half bad although I still think it's kind of a weird concept, covering fruit with chocolate. Except for strawberries. Lovers in movies always feed each other the most wonderful chocolate-covered strawberries. Big, red, juicy—"

"Eeeoooo," April wailed. "I hate it when they do that and then they kiss while they're still eating. Gross beyond words. All I can think of is that they're going to get some of that food in each other's mouth. Yuck."

"You've been married way too long," Teri observed.

"It's those babies. You get overly concerned with germs when you have children," Leigh Ann said.

"Making sure your children don't eat off the floor or lick the carpet is not getting overly concerned about germs," April insisted.

"Gross adult behavior aside, the killer obviously knew you were in the house," April pointed out to Jennifer. "He made sure you wouldn't be able to help her, and I'm glad. Considering the carnage you described to us, if you'd walked in on it, there most likely would have been two more victims: Muffy and yourself. But getting back to Leigh Ann's point, the murderer was careful to avoid a confrontation with you. He had to somehow pass you that night because he had to get back up those stairs. He could have been on the landing or just inside a doorway when you went into Mrs. Ashton's room. How else could he get up there to take the block away?"

Jennifer had tried her best not to dwell on that point. The moment she discovered the wedge gone, she knew it, too. The murderer was still in the house when she made it out of Juliet's room.

"I don't think anyone passed me," Jennifer said simply.

Leigh Ann beamed. "Are you saying—"

"No, I'm not. I think there are other ways to get around in that house."

"So now we're on to secret passages?" Teri let out a loud huff of air. "I don't suppose you saw any oil paintings with moving eyes."

"I'm not talking about anything that sinister. When that house was built, the political situation was unsettled. People did sometimes include secret rooms or ways of getting around."

"Is that how you think the body was transported," April asked, "down some back passageway?"

"All I'm saying is whoever killed Mary Ashton had to be familiar with the house. I'm convinced I would have heard something if the body had been taken down those stairs."

"I knew it! Didn't I tell you even before you went

there? Melba, the housekeeper." Leigh Ann puffed out her chest and rewarded herself with another handful of raisins.

"What I can't figure out is why the murderer took the body away," April said thoughtfully. She opened the banana chips, tried one, and turned to Leigh Ann. "These would definitely be better dipped in chocolate."

"What happened to the body has been bothering me, too," Jennifer confessed. "The murderer had to know the police would identify the victim through the blood, and it's obvious a murder took place. He didn't even try to clean up the room. So what did removing it accomplish?"

"Must have been some kind of evidence on it," Leigh Ann suggested, opening a second can of soda. It hissed at her and sprayed a thin film of sugar water. She grabbed a napkin and wiped it up.

"I bet she let that sucker have it," Teri suggested. "Scratched the bloody heck out of him. If someone came at me with a knife, I'd fight him, whether I had a weapon or not. Get me a little DNA so the police would have something to work with. I might go down, but I'd make sure that suspect they were looking for had something to identify him, like scratches on his face."

Anyone crazy enough to attack Teri would definitely get the worst of it.

"The police didn't find any other blood at the scene, only Mary's," Jennifer told them. "If she did fight back, she didn't do any real damage."

"Skin under her fingernails, then, like Teri said." Leigh Ann nodded. "And the perpetrator didn't have time to get rid of it. If you heard Mary scream through the floor, I'm sure he heard you screaming from above. You say you hollered at the door and then out the window. He had to know you were awake and would find some way to get out."

Jennifer shook her head. "No. They planned to dispose of the body all along. They couldn't have gotten it out of the room without spreading blood all over the place unless they'd brought something to contain it. So why did they take it?"

"For a souvenir?" Leigh Ann suggested.

"You all are giving me indigestion," April declared, closing the bag of chips and securing it with a clothespin.

"Work with me here, Leigh Ann," Jennifer insisted, ignoring April.

She shrugged. "That's what those psychos do in those books, only they usually work alone. You started saying 'they.'"

"That's the problem with having no genderless pronoun for a single person," Jennifer pointed out. "But I'm convinced it was more than one killer. I would have heard someone drag the body from the room. Mary wasn't huge, but a dead body is difficult to manipulate, no matter what its size, even for a strong man. We take for granted how much assistance a live person gives us when we move them."

"So if removing the body didn't have anything to do with the assailant . . ." Leigh Ann began.

"It had to do with Mary." Jennifer shrugged.

"What about fingerprints?" April suggested. She reached across the table and swiped the few remaining chocolate raisins back from Leigh Ann. Apparently she didn't need an appetite to eat them.

"We *know* who she is," Teri pointed out. "They left *all* of her blood behind."

April threw Teri a disgusted look. "I meant on her throat or skin. I think I read somewhere that they can actually get prints off a victim's skin."

"Tricky at best," Jennifer assured her. "I hardly think a murderer is going to be thinking about that. Besides, he'd be wearing gloves, don't you think? And I'm sure he didn't choke her, not with a knife in his hands. But what if the murderer took the body because he wanted to hide something that could have been discovered during an autopsy?"

"If I were writing this," Leigh Ann said, letting her legs drop and leaning forward on the table, "I'd put scars on her pelvis to show she'd had children, children no one knew about."

Teri groaned. "That's soooo unrealistic."

But was it? Was there some physical evidence on the body, some scar, some disease, past or present, that the murderer wanted concealed? Mary didn't marry Shelby until she was at least thirty-one or so. A person could do a lot of living in those years.

"You may be onto something," Jennifer told her.

Leigh Ann threw her a skeptical look as though she hadn't expected anyone to believe her and then warmed to her theory. "I don't mean she had a gaggle of kids, but what if she had one who came back to find her and murder her for deserting him years before. Twins, maybe. That would give you two suspects working together."

Jennifer rolled her eyes. "Okay, now you just went over the edge. What I meant was you're right in that Mary had a life before she met Shelby. And we need to find out what it was."

"We?" Teri asked. "Is that the royal 'we' or are you volunteering our services without asking us first?"

"I was thinking more of the collective we as in I might need you to do a little research for me."

"I don't see how what happened to that woman before

any of us were born could have any bearing on why she was killed now," Teri insisted.

"I don't mean research the past," Jennifer said.

The doorbell rang, and Muffy ducked out from under Teri's hand to help Jennifer answer it. It was Monique. She didn't even bother to say hello, totally ignored Muffy who seemed certain Monique had come just to see her, and thrust a newspaper into Jennifer's hand.

"Sorry I'm late. I was held up. Have you seen this?"

Jennifer opened the page. It was a copy of the free city paper, folded to Malcolm Reed's column. Next to his picture on the left was a headline that read "Ding, Dong, the Witch is Dead."

"If you think Eileen was the only person who hated Mary, you'd better read this article."

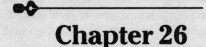

# Chapter 26

Jennifer shut the door and leaned back against it, scanning Malcolm Reed's article.

"Out loud," Terry hollered from her spot on the floor. "There aren't any psychics here."

" 'Black-hearted Mary Ashton left this earth none too soon during the wee hours of Tuesday morning when she was brutally murdered in her own bed. This once prominent Macon socialite finally received her just deserts—' "

"Can we all say the word 'slander'?" Leigh Ann threw out.

"Good question. Can you slander the dead?" Teri asked, staring at Monique.

"No, and even if you could, who would sue on Mary's behalf?" April asked.

Monique collapsed on the sofa, Teri at her feet, having none of the conversation. The last few days had taken their toll. She looked like hell.

"I would if they'd let me keep the settlement," Teri offered.

"That article's not all that's bothering me." Monique leaned forward.

"Has something happened?" Jennifer asked, tossing the article on the table and following Monique to sit on the sofa arm.

"Mary's lawyer called Eileen."

"What for?"

"She's the executor."

"The lawyer?" April asked.

"No." Monique threw them all a work-with-me look. "Mary named Eileen McEvoy executor of her will."

"You're kidding." Jennifer slid off the sofa arm, joining Teri on the floor. "That makes no sense."

"It gets worse. Mary left her the house and everything in it, all of her worldly possessions. Eileen is Mary's sole heir."

"There's your motive," April offered. "It's a heck of a lot stronger than just not liking someone."

"No lie. We're talking big bucks," Teri added.

"Nothing to Arthur?" Jennifer asked.

"Nothing."

"And to Melba?"

"Not a mention."

"So what's she going to do?" Jennifer asked.

"You mean before she goes to prison?" Teri threw in.

"Eileen called Melba immediately and asked her to stay on and continue to take care of the property. And she told her to allow Arthur full use of the kitchen until further notice, although Melba protested that. Eileen doesn't want to put him out of business even though she can't keep him on as a salaried employee."

"This makes no sense to me at all," Jennifer said. "Did Eileen know?"

"Of course not," Monique insisted.

"The police will never believe she didn't." Jennifer ran her hands through her hair, totally confused. "Mary Ashton told me she suspected Eileen was the one behind those threats. She also told me they'd been going on for some time. Why would she make plans to have someone, namely me, document them and not even bother to change her will?"

"She did change her will, eight months ago, only the change was to make Eileen the beneficiary," Monique told her.

"About the time of the competency hearing," Jennifer observed.

"I don't know why you all seem confused. It makes perfect sense to me," Leigh Ann announced.

"Of course it would." Teri threw her a sly look. "So let's hear this 'perfect' sense."

"If Mary knew Eileen was trying to take the property away from her, if she considered Eileen a threat, making her the beneficiary might have been her way of appeasing her. She might have been saying, 'Look, I'll make sure the property stays in the family. You can have it. Just wait until I die.' "

"But if she kept it to herself, and Eileen didn't know—" April began.

"We only have Eileen's word that she didn't know she was the beneficiary," Jennifer pointed out. "One private phone call would have been all it would take."

"Eileen's word is good enough for me." Monique threw Jennifer a challenging look.

"But whether she knew it or not is actually irrelevant," Jennifer indicated. "The only thing that matters is that the police, who are already suspicious of Eileen, are going to say she had one heck of a motive for murder."

"But why not just wait until Mary died?" April asked again.

"Maybe Eileen wanted it settled before her own death," Teri suggested. "She was older than Mary by several years. Once she died, she had no guarantee that her children would inherit, that Mary wouldn't change her will again. Maybe she just couldn't take it one more day. Maybe she simply wanted everything settled once and for all."

Monique stood and grabbed her purse. "Eileen McEvoy did not kill Mary Ashton. If you all insist on speculating as to how and why she did it, I'll thank you kindly *not* to do it in my presence." She went straight to the door without even a glance at any of them.

"Monique . . ." Jennifer began.

But Monique already had the door open. She shot a look at Jennifer and then shut the door behind her.

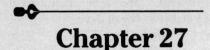

# Chapter 27

Jennifer leaned over the back of her sofa, worked her fingers up and down Sam's neck, and whispered in his ear, "What do you know about Malcolm Reed?"

Immediately, she felt his muscles tense back up as his eyes snapped open.

"I knew it!" he said, pulling out of her grip and twisting to look at her.

"What?" she asked, all innocence.

"I know you don't have an off switch, but can't you relax for even one evening? What did you do all day? Stew?"

"I tried not to. I made some salads for Dee Dee and froze them."

"I didn't think she served anything frozen."

"Normally she doesn't, but she has too much work for all of us to get done on time, and I suggested some recipes that do really well. I promised her no one will ever know the difference."

"Good. Did you get any writing done?"

"A little."

"And did you keep any of those pages?"

She shook her head. She'd wadded them up and thrown them away.

"Of course you didn't. You get some fool thought in your mind and you won't let it go, not even for two minutes. You were thinking about it all through dinner, too, weren't you?"

"I simply asked you a question."

"You made me my favorite meal. You bought my favorite wine. You even rubbed my neck. I should have suspected something was up, something other than what I hoped."

"I'm sorry. I didn't mean to break the mood."

"Jennifer . . ."

"Okay. I already apologized. Forget I said anything." She slipped in next to him on the sofa and snuggled up against him, playing with the buttons on his shirt. They sat there for several minutes, neither uttering a sound, their breathing falling into rhythm. He put his arm around her, but then she felt his chest heave. Maybe if he couldn't forgive her, she could at least help him forget.

She started at his ear and planted little kisses down his jaw. Then she cupped his face in her hands, turned him toward her, closed her eyes, and kissed him as though she hadn't seen him in a long, long time because in a real way, she hadn't.

What? Was she crazy? Sam was right. They didn't get enough time alone together. The heck with Mary Ashton, Juliet, and Malcolm. One night wouldn't make any difference to any of them, especially as two of them were dead. Suddenly she couldn't imagine why she had thought it would.

Sam swung her gently around, their lips never losing contact, cradling her in his lap. Finally, when they came up for air, he hugged her to him, tightly, possessively. She could have stayed like that forever, all thoughts of whatever it was she'd been thinking—at the moment she couldn't quite remember what it was—completely gone from her mind. All she cared about was Sam. Sweet, delicious, incredibly sexy Sam.

He nuzzled her ear, nipping at it. "What's your interest in Malcolm Reed?"

And he had the nerve to talk about her not letting things go. Curiosity killed a lot more than cats.

She drew back and stared at him. At times, they were way too much alike. "It can wait."

"Are you kidding? It's like Reed's right here between the two of us."

If he was, *she* certainly hadn't noticed.

"Let's get it out of the way so we can get back to . . ."

She paused, waiting to see if he would get back to what they'd been doing, but he didn't. He just sat there, staring down at her. It was her fault. She'd brought it up in the first place. Better to deal with Reed and be done with it.

She bounced up, took the newspaper Monique had brought to her off the table, plopped it in his lap, and then rejoined him. "His girlfriend died almost thirty years ago, and he still hated her stepmother so much he wrote a column comparing her to the Wicked Witch of the East. He used to go with Juliet Ashton."

Sam leaned back, folding his arms across his chest. "Now *that* I didn't know. Malcolm has a few, shall we say, unresolved issues."

"No lie. Anybody who ever read anything he's written could tell that. So what do you know?"

"He comes from a monied Atlanta family, who, most likely, has nothing to do with him. I understand he lives in a run-down bungalow in the middle of nowhere. Dropped out of college, if what I heard is correct, sometime in the Sixties. You can tell he never trained as a journalist if you read his stuff because he never quite developed an ear for it. He doesn't follow the rules, not in his life and not in his work."

"Still a hippie?" she marveled. "They're getting rare."

"I don't know if you could call him that, but he never gave up protesting, although what he protests changes. I suspect he lives on family money. I wouldn't think that free paper he owns could bring in enough to keep him in the squalor I understand he enjoys."

"He owns that paper?" She was genuinely surprised.

"How else do you think he could get away with the things he says in it?"

"I attributed it to free speech."

"Attribute it to self-publication." Sam shook his head, a grin threatening the corners of his mouth. She hated it when he acted as though she were naive because she wasn't. She simply had a more optimistic view of life than he did.

"Is he married?"

"Not that I know of. He's quite a character. All the reporters talk about him. Could be a little envy, I suppose, on some base, subhuman level, for all that freedom. I understand he's had a succession of live-in lady friends."

"Really?"

"Yeah. He adheres to the love-the-one-you're-with philosophy."

"Could he still be carrying a torch for Juliet?" she asked.

"I doubt it. I think he simply has no respect for the legal system. Can't imagine what a woman would see in him anyway."

Jennifer always found that interesting: how a man often couldn't see what a woman found attractive in a man who didn't fit the accepted image of handsome or successful. But this Reed character sounded like he made it hard to understand for a whole lot of reasons. Men who hadn't settled down by middle age generally lost their promise as fixer-uppers. By then, the charm was gone. Yet there always seemed to be some woman out there willing to take them on. At least for a while.

"What's the article say, other than calling Mary Ashton names?" Sam asked.

"That Macon can now rest easy since the house has finally dropped on one of its master manipulators."

"I see. And was she wearing red-and-white striped stockings when she died? Do you know if Mary had a reputation as a manipulator?"

"If she did, Monique didn't mention it, although she was certainly strong willed. Mary seemed to keep her sphere of influence fairly close, within the walls of the Ashton mansion, at least during the last several years."

"Affecting . . ."

"Most notably Shelby, who's dead; Juliet, who's dead; Melba, presumably alive; and Arthur, definitely alive. And, by association, Malcolm Reed, Eileen McEvoy, and Eileen's family. But surely Malcolm hasn't had anything to do with her since Juliet died. Why would he?"

"I wouldn't give Malcolm's rantings too much credence. He's got a lot of anger. Give him any convenient object, system, or person to direct it at and he's right there."

"My point exactly. Whoever killed Mary had a lot of anger."

"Let's say he did kill her since you seem so intent on exploring a completely unfounded possibility. Why would he wait so long? The woman wasn't young, and his girlfriend, if that's where the hatred comes from, died years ago."

Jennifer sighed and plopped down, deflating.

"She *was* a manipulator, you know," Sam said.

Jennifer swiveled her head toward him. "How so?"

"She did a number on you."

"What do you mean?"

"She manipulated you into staying with her. When one tactic didn't work, namely money, she appealed to your conscience. One short conversation with you, and she had you pegged."

Jennifer nodded. As much as she hated to admit it, he was right. She'd even known it when it was happening, but people like that are hard to resist.

"She was so good at it," he went on, "that here you are trying to figure out who killed her."

"She made me promise."

"I rest my case."

"What did you find out at the courthouse?"

"The only address for Mary listed on the marriage license was the Ashton mansion," Sam said.

Jennifer perked back up. "Okay. That definitely puts her living in the house *before* she married Shelby."

"Right. Free to work her wiles on Shelby and to convince him that she was invaluable in Juliet's life. From what you've told me, Juliet was Shelby's weakness."

Jennifer nodded. Now that she'd learned more about Mary, that explanation was far more likely than Shelby simply falling in love with his daughter's attractive caretaker.

"Did the license list her place of birth?"

"Charleston, South Carolina."

"I don't suppose you were able to get a social security number."

"Yeah, but don't ask me how I did it."

She knew exactly how he got it. Charm. It served him well. He also had a way of asking questions that made people think they were correcting or confirming instead of offering new information. And it didn't hurt that he could read upside down.

"She didn't apply for a number until she went to work for Ashton," Sam told her. "In 1959 you didn't need one until you got a legitimate job, not like now when you come out of the womb with one. Shelby wasn't paying Mary under the table. She actually did have a salary and not a bad one for the time. Once she married him, however, her account went inactive."

"You mean she didn't work anymore."

"Right. And she never tried to draw on it. She hadn't worked more than two quarters."

"Interesting. So she didn't have a job before she hired on as Clarisse Ashton's nurse, at least not a professional one. I wonder if he knew that. She had to supply him with some references, don't you think?"

"His wife was ill. I'm sure he was distracted, and he probably needed someone right away."

"Right," she agreed. "Could have made him careless, just when he needed to be especially careful. And then after she married Shelby, she had access to more money than she could possibly spend, so it's no big surprise she didn't work then. I wouldn't either if I had that kind of money."

"Sure, you would. You'd write."

"I'm glad you think that's work. Some people don't, you know."

He grinned. "I do it every day. They even pay me for it." He realized the moment the words left his mouth what he'd said.

"Someday someone will pay me for it, too," she told him.

"I've never once doubted it," he assured her.

She hated it when they talked about her writing. He was so understanding she felt like every rejection she received was a personal affront to him, as if she were failing him as well as herself. And his kindness was almost as painful to accept. But she was getting better at it.

"I talked to April on the phone today."

"Yeah? What's she up to?"

"She's waiting for her contract to come in the mail, and she's putting together a proposal for another couple of books. Her editor liked her pitches over the phone. She's almost sure to take them."

"She deserves it," Sam said.

"Absolutely," Jennifer agreed.

"So do you."

Better to change the subject. "I called Monique this morning and apologized to her. I haven't been as careful as I should about my comments when she's around. These people are her family."

"So how did she respond?" Sam asked.

"You know Monique. She's hard to read, but I guess we're okay. I asked if there was anything I could do for her, and she said she'd like me to notify Mary's next of kin."

"In South Carolina?"

"I guess. I don't know where else to look. I'll drop by Eileen's tomorrow and see if she has any information that might help me."

"Good."

"So are we done now?" she asked.

He knocked the newspaper to the floor, grabbed her hand and kissed it. "We have yet to begin."

She grinned. Maybe she hadn't ruined the night after all.

# Chapter 28

"Mary never spoke of her family," Eileen assured Jennifer, amid shades of cream and ice blue in the elegant sunroom of the McEvoy home. Sleek, modern, bright, with a whole wall of windows facing a forest of pecan trees—such a contrast to the gloom of the Ashton mansion. "I don't believe she mentioned them more than once in all the years I knew her. All she said was that her parents were dead. I assumed she had no siblings. She never spoke of any, and no one on her side even came to the wedding. I never gave it much thought. The type of work she was doing led me to assume she didn't have strong ties anywhere. I'm ashamed to say I didn't think about contacting anyone about her death. Can I offer you a cookie?"

Eileen lifted a silver tray spread with homemade pecan sandies rolled in powdered sugar. Silver in a sunroom. This woman lived in a different world.

Jennifer accepted one and took a small bite. Her mouth was so dry, she could barely taste it, but she felt it rude to refuse. She took a napkin and dabbed at the sugar she felt clinging to her lips, then quickly took a sip of her iced tea. "So you don't have an address for any of her relations."

"I'm afraid I don't even have a name to suggest to you, except for her family name of Bedford." She sat the tray back down, not taking any cookies for herself. "I must say I was surprised when you called this morning and asked to see me."

Jennifer really wanted to ask Eileen about being Mary's beneficiary, but she knew not to push it, not quite yet. She had to gain the woman's trust, to work into it gently, to demonstrate some sensitivity and some manners.

"I don't think you murdered Mary," Jennifer confessed honestly. It wasn't what she'd intended to say, but it'd come out anyway.

Eileen offered a mirthless smile. "You truly are naive, aren't you?"

That comment made Jennifer blush.

"I don't mean to embarrass you," Eileen went on, "but we're all capable of murder under the proper circumstances. If you're telling me this to win me over," she raised an eyebrow at Jennifer, "I assure you I don't intend to tell you anything I wouldn't tell anyone else who asked. Would you care for another cookie?"

Jennifer shook her head, refusing the sweet. "Actually, I simply meant that if you had killed her, I would have expected you to do it with a good deal more grace and style. She was family after all."

For the first time, Jennifer saw true amusement in Eileen's face.

"Do you know how Shelby met Mary?" Jennifer asked.

"No, now that you mention it. She was working for him, as you know, but I don't think he ever said how he found her. I wouldn't be surprised if she'd simply shown up on his doorstep, and he let her in, like a stray cat."

"Wasn't she competent?"

"She seemed aware of the drugs and doses the doctor prescribed for Clarisse's care. I presume that required a basic knowledge of the written word and an acquaintance with teaspoons and fractions thereof."

"And what about after Clarisse died?"

"She stayed on. Melba wanted to handle Juliet along with the house, but it was too much for her. That child was such a lively little thing. Cute as a button, but, my, what a handful! I offered to take her, at least for a while, but Shelby couldn't bear to be separated from her, and Mary assured him she was well versed in child care.

"That house takes a lot of management," Eileen went on. "When Clarisse was alive, they had a crew to maintain it and to help with all of their social obligations, but most of that stopped when Clarisse fell ill. Her attacks became frequent and unpredictable. She was terrified of surgery. I suppose that's why she died. She put it off and put it off, ignoring the doctor's warnings. Finally, she went to his office for an appointment, doubled over in pain, and he wouldn't let her go home. Had an ambulance come and take her straight over. Scared all of us to death. And then when they finally released her from the hospital, she was so weak."

"And that's when Mary came in."

"Mary let a lot of the help go when she took over her care." Eileen took a quick sip of tea. "And then later, after Shelby died, she fired everyone except Melba and Arthur. I think she would have let Melba go if she'd thought she could find anyone else who could do the job."

"Did Juliet ever mention anyone named Tiffany or Darren?"

"Not that I recall. Why ever would you ask me that? Is it important?"

"I don't know."

"She had lots of friends here and at school, but I

wouldn't know who they were. She never really confided in me."

"But you did know that she was involved with Malcolm Reed," Jennifer said.

"Against her father's wishes."

"Why?"

"Have you ever read any of his work? He publishes that dreadful free paper that's handed out on the street."

Jennifer nodded.

"The man's a beast. Totally untrained in any sort of etiquette."

"Then why did Juliet—"

"Oh, I suppose he did have a certain amount of charisma in his youth, at least for that era, and I'm sure he was unlike anyone she'd ever known before. That, in itself, seems to hold some charm for you young people. But, as I said, he had no sense of decorum, no respect for mores, for virtues, certainly not for people, except maybe Juliet and even then. . . . Back in the Sixties, all that free love nonsense. My children were young then, too.

"Shelby had quite a battle on his hands. Juliet would try to slip out sometimes in the middle of the night. I suspect they didn't know where she was half the time, but that's the way it is with most teenagers, isn't it? You think they're up in their rooms reading and heaven only knows where they're off to and what they're doing. And with whom."

"Are you saying that Shelby was fearful about Juliet's relationship with Malcolm?" Talking about sex to someone like Eileen was almost impossible. She had no idea what words to use.

"Not just Shelby. Mary, too. I didn't agree with her methods—she seemed determined to put a stop to it—but she seemed to want what was best for Juliet. Even if it wasn't always what Juliet wanted."

Eileen glanced at her watch.

"Am I keeping you?" Jennifer asked.

"I have to go by the house today. We'll have to begin an inventory as soon as possible. As you can see, I've found myself saddled with Mary's affairs."

"So I heard."

"Somehow I suspected you had. You seem far more interested in all this than can possibly be good for you."

"Did you know she'd left it all to you, before her death, I mean?"

"If I said no, would you believe me?"

"What will become of the property now?"

"I'd like to create a foundation for its preservation. I can't imagine anyone in the family wanting to live there, especially now. Is that it?"

"One more thing. How much do you trust Melba?"

She'd crossed the line. Eileen's face clearly told her so. "I have far more reason to trust her than I do you."

"The night Mary was killed," Jennifer rushed on, "I think that someone may have—"

The doorbell gave out a series of chimes, distracting them both. A few seconds later, the housekeeper ushered Nicholls and two officers into the room. His eyes narrowed when he saw Jennifer.

Both women stood. "Lieutenant Nicholls," Eileen began. "You're back. I thought your officers had finished their work yesterday. Is there something more—"

"Mrs. Eileen Ashton McEvoy," he interrupted.

This sounded way too formal to be comfortable.

"You know very well who I am. Why are you—"

"You're under arrest for the murder of Mary Bedford Ashton. You have the right to remain silent. You have the right to speak to an attorney and to have an attorney present—"

Mrs. McEvoy's eyes grew huge, but other than that she remained calm and seemingly in complete control. She put a none-too-steady hand on Jennifer's arm. "Call my daughter. And my lawyer. Tell them to get down to the police station. Now."

Nicholls continued to Mirandize Mrs. McEvoy as he led her out of the room, leaving Jennifer staring after them, wondering what could possibly have happened to allow the police to make the leap from suspicion to arrest.

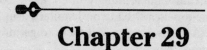

# Chapter 29

"They found a knife with Mary's blood and hair on it, wrapped in a piece of silk and buried in Eileen's rose garden," Sam told Jennifer.

She sat where he had found her, on the hood of his Honda in the *Telegraph* parking lot, watching the sun sink lower in the sky.

"Pale green silk with flowers on it," Jennifer said more to herself than to him.

"That's right. How did you know?"

"That was her nightgown, the one Mary was wearing the night she died. Any fingerprints?"

"None." He offered her a hand, and she slid off to stand next to him.

"There are better places to wait for me," he told her. "Why didn't you come up?"

"I didn't want to bother you again at the office, but I knew you'd know why the police arrested Mrs. McEvoy. I also knew you'd have to leave eventually, and I didn't think you could do it without your car."

"You're right about that."

"How did they get permission to search her grounds?" Jennifer asked. "Surely they didn't have enough evidence for a warrant."

"Eileen gave it to them."

"Then she couldn't have known it was there. She isn't that stupid."

"But maybe the person she hired is," Sam suggested with one of his knowing grins.

"Okay, then maybe she did do it," Jennifer said. "It's certainly the simplest solution and apparently one everyone seems dead set on going with: woman hates sister-in-law, waits until brother dies, can't achieve control of family mansion through the courts, makes threats, then resorts to the oldest form of righting wrongs, brute force. Only the mansion was willed to her. What was there to fight over?"

Jennifer threw up her hands and started to pace.

"Stop fretting. It's not good for you," Sam told her, opening the rear door and tossing his briefcase and his jacket onto the backseat.

She circled back around his car. "You don't want me to stop, not really. I get mean when I don't have an outlet."

"Then by all means," Sam waved his hand at her to proceed. He added his tie to the pile and then shut the door.

She was being rude and she knew it. But he wasn't much better. "What should we do?"

"And why do you think we should do anything?" Sam asked.

Wrong answer.

"Don't give me that. This is all crazy. I know in my bones Eileen didn't kill Mary."

"Since when?" Sam asked.

"Since . . . since right now. Since you said that we shouldn't do anything to help her."

"The police will find out who killed Mrs. Ashton," Sam assured her, leaning against the door.

She shook her head at him. She believed in the police

as much as he did, but the threats against Mary had been a little too convenient. What if Mary had been wrong? What if someone else had planted those notes? And the knife? What if someone was trying to frame Eileen? "I'm going to see Malcolm Reed. He's as likely a suspect as Eileen."

"Wait just a minute." Sam warned her. "I don't want you anywhere around him. He's nuts."

"Exactly my point."

"I mean it. Stay away from him." He put a hand on her arm, but she shrugged it off.

"What would you have me do?" she asked.

"Nothing. Like I said, the police are perfectly competent. So are Eileen's attorneys, I'm sure, and her daughter. If you can't stand it—"

"I can't. A woman like that shouldn't be locked up in a cell. It makes my skin crawl just to think about it."

"She's already been released on bond. Did you think her daughter the judge would allow her mother to spend any time in jail?"

"No, I suppose not."

"Look. You need to find something to do besides fretting about Eileen. Didn't you promise Monique you'd find Mary's people in South Carolina and let them know she's dead? Maybe they'll have some insight to offer. That's something you can do tonight—without leaving your apartment."

"This is busy work, something to keep me occupied," she pouted.

He grinned at her. "It's something that needs to be done, should have been done days ago. And, if it happens to keep you out of trouble, all the better."

"I don't go looking for it, you know."

"I know. That makes me even more uneasy." He pulled a folded piece of paper out of his pocket and handed it to her. "I had Charleston County fax me a copy of Mary's birth certificate. It's not much, but maybe you can use her parents' names to track down her next of kin. At least you'll be doing something for Mary, and it'll give me some time to find out more about what the police have put together."

She unfolded it and looked at it. "There's no address or anything on here, only a place of birth for her parents."

"Right. Seems they stayed settled where she was born. Maybe the rest of her family did, too."

She nodded. In the best of all possible worlds, they'd been a close family and some great-niece or nephew was named after one of them. If not, she could always go down the entire list of Bedfords in Charleston, asking if any of them had ever heard of Mary or her parents. At least the net made it easier. Maybe she'd get lucky.

"That's right. Mary Elizabeth Bedford. She moved to Macon, Georgia, in the Fifties and married Shelby Ashton. . . . Her parents were Fiona and Adlai. . . . You haven't? All right. Thank you."

Jennifer dropped the receiver back into its cradle and drew a heavy black line through Bedford, Leonard. Her phone bill was growing larger with each ring. At least it wouldn't be due until next month.

She scooped the phone back up and punched in the number for Bedford, Otis. A woman greeted her with a "Good evening" in that distinctive coastal accent unique to Charleston.

"I was hoping you could help me find someone," Jennifer began. "I'm looking for relatives of Mary Elizabeth Bedford." She paused, expecting the same "I've never heard of her" she'd gotten in the last three calls, but the woman said nothing. "She's the daughter of Fiona and Adlai Bedford."

"Yes," was all the woman said.

Yes did not constitute an acknowledgment, Jennifer reminded herself, trying not to get excited. She squeezed her eyes shut and said a little prayer. "You know who she is?"

"Yes," the woman repeated.

"She was born Christmas Eve of 1929."

"Yes."

"Are you a relative?" Jennifer asked.

"By marriage," the woman said.

"Well, I have some bad news for you. I'm afraid she's dead."

"You don't say," the woman said.

No regret, no remorse. What was that in the woman's voice? A little amused curiosity? She was, after all, only a relative by marriage.

"I just thought the family should be notified," Jennifer told her, at once regretting her phone bill.

Again the pause.

"Are you there?" Jennifer ventured. And then she heard a slight snuffle over the line. The woman seemed to be stifling a laugh.

"Land's sake. I never would have believed she'd last this long," the woman said.

"She was getting along in years, but people live to be a lot older. Did she have a medical condition?" Jennifer babbled.

"That's not what I meant," the woman insisted, her voice cracking a bit. Jennifer suspected she must be close to Mary's age, especially if she remembered her. "I just thought someone would have killed that witch long before now."

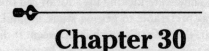

# Chapter 30

"Sam wouldn't go with you, huh?" Leigh Ann stated, tossing a Macon map over her shoulder to Teri, who was stretched out across the entire backseat of the little Beetle. Jennifer watched in the rearview mirror as it dropped toward Teri's bare legs. It was way too hot for anything but shorts.

"My money says he has no idea what Miss Jennifer here is up to. He's obviously got more sense than we do and better ways to spend a Saturday morning," Teri said, opening the folded paper and obscuring her head from Jennifer's view. "Didn't you learn to read maps in school, Leigh Ann?"

"Sure," Leigh Ann insisted, "but once we're off pavement I get all confused with those tiny black lines, and none of these roads are marked."

"Sure they are," Teri told her. "See that number on that post?"

It whipped past.

"That was a road number?" Leigh Ann asked, craning her neck. "They actually expect you to read signs like that?"

"Just keep on like you're going," Teri instructed Jennifer. "We've got at least a mile or two to go yet before our next turn."

"What exactly did that woman who was related to

**161**

Mary tell you over the phone?" Leigh Ann asked, settling back in her seat.

Jennifer checked her rearview mirror, this time to look at the road. They were kicking up a lot of red dust, but then dust was preferable to getting stuck in mud. On a road like that, there wasn't much in between. If they got caught in one of Macon's typical heat-breaking downpours, they might just find themselves slogging their way back through it.

"She said Mary hadn't seen or spoken to anyone in her family for more than forty years," Jennifer answered.

"Never once contacted them?" Teri asked, her dark eyes appearing above the edge of the map.

"Not once."

"And you expected them to feel warm and fuzzy toward her?" Teri snorted. "If my mom didn't hear from me, assuming I ever get to move out of her house, she'd let me know on a regular basis that I was falling down on my familial obligations."

"But that's your mama. I got the impression Mary's family was just as glad to see her go, no questions asked. Mrs. Bedford assured me she had no intention of kicking in any money for the burial expenses." Jennifer rolled her window up. She had no air conditioning in her car, but she could deal better with heat than with the dirt that was blowing in.

"What'd this relative have to say about her?" Leigh Ann asked, letting the wind whip through her hair. "What kind of crap did she pull for them to cut her loose like that?"

"She said Mary was always interfering in everyone's life, that she had this uncanny way of finding out things." The car hit a rut, and they all bounced and came down hard.

"Time for new shocks," Teri pointed out.

"It's on the list," Jennifer assured her. It just wasn't high on the list.

"Reading mail, listening at doors, spending a lot of time thinking about what was none of her business," Leigh Ann suggested. "It's easy to pick up on what's going on around you if you take the time."

"Spoken like a pro," Teri mumbled from the back, then piped up. "Deductive reasoning isn't so much a talent as it is simple observation. So what did Mary do with this information she gathered?"

"That's a no-brainer," Leigh Ann said. "Do you know who she was blackmailing?"

Jennifer pulled the car hard to the left to avoid a large rock in the road. "Technically, I don't think it was blackmail. No money was involved. She was after—"

"Power," Teri finished. "Once money is spent, it's gone. But power—now that's a much more lasting pleasure."

"Teri!" Leigh Ann chastised.

"I was speaking theoretically, of course. I take it she ultimately chose the wrong person to screw over."

"Yep," Jennifer said. "Her uncle. Seems they were a little too much alike. He gave her twenty-four hours to clear out. She never looked back but why should she? She came to Macon and got herself hired into the household of one of the city's premiere families on the pretext of being a nurse."

"You mean she wasn't?" Leigh Ann asked.

"She didn't even finish high school according to the woman I spoke with. However she managed it, by chance or by plan, she found herself conveniently available to take Clarisse Ashton's place after she died."

"Do you hear what you're saying?" Teri asked. "Are you implying she had something to do with—"

"I'm simply saying she took advantage of a situation,"

Jennifer assured her. "No reason to believe it was any more than that, at least not at this point."

"Yeah? Well, deep down, I think she loved Shelby," Leigh Ann said.

"You would," Teri said.

"She stayed," Leigh Ann pointed out.

"Of course she stayed. She didn't have any 'up' to go to from being Mrs. Shelby Ashton," Teri pointed out.

"My mama always says it's just as easy to fall in love with a rich man as it is a poor man," Leigh Ann added.

"Yeah? So why didn't *she*?" Jennifer asked.

Leigh Ann gave her a puzzled look. "I don't know. Next time I see her, I'll ask."

"Turn here," Teri shouted out, as they passed a turnoff to the left.

Jennifer stopped the car. "That doesn't even look like a road."

"You have to trust the navigator," Teri insisted.

"Why?" Leigh Ann asked.

"Because if you don't, she'll stop navigating."

"You better do what she says, Jennifer," Leigh Ann warned, "because if she gives me back the map, we're goners."

Jennifer backed the car up and made the turn. "There's no sign."

"It's the first black line after that last intersection. It doesn't have a number on the map. I think it may be private property."

"I'm beginning to wish we'd unwound a ball of string." More than the heat was getting to Jennifer. "Even if we do find this place, I'm not at all sure we'll be able to find our way back out."

The trees on either side of the narrow road were tall, offering some small respite to the heat. Wire fencing tacked onto makeshift posts ran along either side, but if there was livestock in those fields, they couldn't see them. They probably had enough sense to find a nice cool pond or at least the shade of a large oak tree to lie in.

"I don't think it's too much further," Teri told her. "The line runs out just up this way a little, right where you drew that circle on the map. Who'd you get these directions from anyway?"

"Ned, down in the morgue at the *Telegraph* office, yesterday afternoon while I was waiting for Sam to get off work."

"I know him," Leigh Ann said. Leigh Ann knew everybody. "I wouldn't take directions from him. He's a little strange."

Maybe someday she'd learn to listen to Sam.

When the unpainted wooden structure came into view, Jennifer stopped the car just outside the open steel gate stretched across the road.

Teri rose up from the back and leaned over the seats between Jennifer and Leigh Ann. "What a dump."

It was indeed a dump. It looked like a cabin that had grown in the most unplanned, unexpected directions. Additions shot off from both sides of the main, two-story midsection. The wood, never painted, had been allowed to weather to an ugly gray. Stone steps led up to the only nice portion of the structure, a full porch across the entire front of the original house. Guinea hens fluttered loose around the grassless yard.

"Remind me again why we needed to come out here," Teri said. "I've heard those things peck."

A woman appeared at the door, pushing open the screen. She must have heard the noise from the car. Small and slender, with long dark hair, she wore a tank top and the shortest shorts Jennifer had ever seen this side of Daisy Duke. She gave them all a narrow-eyed stare.

Jennifer opened her car door.

"Don't go up there. I bet she's got dogs," Leigh Ann warned.

"Dogs and hens I can handle. I just hope she doesn't have a shotgun resting inside that door." Jennifer stood, pulling the wrinkles out of her denim shorts, squinting at the sun, and wondering exactly what she was going to say.

Teri pushed the driver's seat forward and climbed out behind her.

"Oh, all right," Leigh Ann grumbled, "but if I get bit, pecked, or shot, I'm holding you responsible."

The woman walked further out onto the porch and stood holding onto one of the wooden supports. Jennifer could see now that she was not much more than a girl, certainly no more than twenty.

Jennifer put on her friendliest smile. "Good morning. We're looking for Malcolm Reed. Is this his place?"

The girl nodded, but the suspicious stare was still there.

Jennifer nodded in rhythm. "Is he in?"

"He's busy. I can take him a message, but it'd better be important. He don't like to be disturbed."

One of those additions must be his home office. Most likely he had the newspaper printed by some company in town.

"All we want is to ask him a few questions," Jennifer assured her.

"What about?"

"Juliet Ashton."

"Why?" the woman asked, her brow wrinkling.

Not who. So she most likely knew who Juliet was, even though she'd obviously been born years after her death.

"You know about Malcolm and Juliet?" Jennifer asked.

The woman shrugged. "That was a long time ago."

"Yes, it was," Jennifer agreed, edging toward her.

"He has me now."

And she—lucky her—had Malcolm.

"Of course he does." What was this girl's IQ? Functional but probably not much better than that.

"Her stepmother was killed and her aunt has been arrested for the murder. Mr. Reed wrote an article about the death and—"

"And what?" a male voice demanded.

Jennifer swung her head to the left. A scraggly figure had come around the side of the building, wearing torn jeans and a Grateful Dead T-shirt. He was, indeed, holding a shotgun, and he looked more than ready to use it.

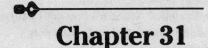

# Chapter 31

"Oh, hell," Teri muttered under her breath, staring straight at Malcolm Reed's finger twitching on the trigger of his shotgun. Leigh Ann stood frozen in what looked like horror.

"Mr. Reed," Jennifer addressed the long-haired, unkempt, middle-aged man. His photo in his newspaper made him look a whole lot better than he did right then. And a whole lot more reasonable. "I'm sure you've heard that Eileen McEvoy, Mary Ashton's sister-in-law, has been accused of her murder."

"What of it?" he demanded.

Teri and Leigh Ann had lined up directly behind Jennifer. Next time she invited someone along, she'd find someone with a little more guts. But, in all fairness, the man did have a crazed look in his eyes. She just hoped he wasn't high. She suspected that he wasn't all that reasonable sober either.

"I've made all the comments I intend to make in my column." He cocked one barrel of the shotgun.

Jennifer opened her hands in front of her. "We're leaving. If you know of anything at all that might help clear Eileen . . . I just wanted to remind you that she did everything she could to help Juliet."

"I guess that just wasn't enough, now was it?"

**168**

"Obviously not, but I still don't understand why she did it, why Juliet killed herself."

"That bitch of a stepmother of hers killed her." He was livid.

"You don't mean that literally," Jennifer insisted.

"Do you?" Leigh Ann piped up from behind.

"I mean it however you want to take it."

"I understand your loss," Jennifer started and then realized her mistake. Grief that deep did not seek sympathy. It lived in a world all its own.

"No you don't. And she didn't just kill herself," Malcolm said, his angry words catching in his throat. "We weren't even together then, so why don't you go talk to someone who cares."

But he did care. His tirade in his newspaper proved that much. So did his demeanor right then.

"Did you ever know a Tiffany or a Darren?" Jennifer asked.

His face turned white. "What kind of games are you playing? Just get the hell off my land," he warned, cocking the other barrel of the gun.

Jennifer, Teri, and Leigh Ann scrambled past the gate for the Beetle, tumbling in as fast as they could. Jennifer gunned the engine, swung the car around, and took off before they could even get their seatbelts on.

In the rearview mirror, Jennifer watched Reed discharge the gun into the air. The man was, indeed, crazy.

"You heard what he said, didn't you?" Jennifer asked, trying to keep at least one eye on the road in front of her.

"Yeah, get the hell out," Teri said. "No one holding a shotgun has to tell me twice."

"Not that. He said she didn't just kill herself."

"Maybe he feels like he died with her," Leigh Ann offered, holding on tightly to the handle above her door.

Jennifer shook her head as they sped down the dirt

road. Without hardly even slowing down, she took a right at the end of the fence and swung onto the next road, spewing dirt and gravel in their wake.

Light had dawned as Malcolm stood there, gun in hand, angry as hell even after all these years. The photo of the two of them—Malcolm and Juliet. The paper with lists of names hidden with it. She'd only risked asking about Tiffany and Darren because she'd had to know for sure, and his reaction left no doubt. Any hatred that Eileen McEvoy had for Mary paled against the emotions that Malcolm Reed still carried with him, would probably always carry with him.

"Have you ever thought about what you'd name your children?" Jennifer asked, gunning the engine once more, the little Beetle courageously straining forward.

"Sure," Leigh Ann said.

"Ever made a list of boys' and girls' names?"

"We're tearing away from some madman with a gun and you're talking about your firstborn-to-be who, I might point out, already has a name?" Teri asked, holding onto the back of the driver's seat as they bounced over the rough ground.

"Ever considered Tiffany or Darren?"

"Of course not. Those are old names," Leigh Ann pointed out.

"Right. Thirty years old."

"Are you saying—" Teri began.

"That's right. I think Juliet was pregnant with Malcolm's child."

"So you mean that's why she killed herself," Teri asked, "because of the shame? Her daddy would have had a fit."

"Yes, he would have but that's not why," Jennifer assured her. "She could have handled him—he loved her so much—and she would have remembered that if someone else hadn't interfered, hadn't convinced her otherwise."

"A child out of wedlock was a big deal in those days," Leigh Ann insisted.

"To some people," Jennifer agreed. "But Malcolm wouldn't care that they weren't married, before or after the child was born. If he didn't, I have a feeling Juliet wouldn't either. He'd celebrate their child."

"But her parents—" Teri started.

"I suspect her father never knew. He never had the chance to tell her it would be all right. God. No wonder Malcolm hated Mary. Snoop and master manipulator, a deadly combination. Juliet must have told him what she'd done, how she solved their 'problem.' He couldn't forgive her, so he left her. And she couldn't forgive herself."

"Do you mind letting us in on exactly what you mean?" Teri rose up between the seats.

"Don't you see?" Jennifer asked. "Mary must have forced Juliet to have an illegal abortion."

"Forced her?" Leigh Ann asked.

"Pressured her, convinced her that her father would have nothing more to do with her," Jennifer corrected. "Juliet wanted that baby."

"Why are you so sure?" Teri asked.

"Because she made a list of names. Because she shared that list with Malcolm. She wouldn't have done that if she wanted an abortion."

"And you think she told Malcolm about the operation," Teri added.

"Yes, but not until after she'd gone through with it."

"And when he found out—" Leigh Ann started.

"All hell broke loose," Teri added.

"And Juliet killed herself," Jennifer finished.

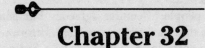

# Chapter 32

"All of it?" Jennifer gasped, staring in disbelief at Monique, Teri, and Leigh Ann in turn.

"Every last penny," Monique assured her. She shut the door to Jennifer's apartment behind her. "Mary mortgaged the house for its full value and took out liens against all of its contents."

They'd barely had time for a glass of lemonade before Monique had come knocking. Leigh Ann and Teri, stretched out on the hardwood floor, too dusty from their trip to the country to be allowed in contact with upholstered furniture, were still sipping on theirs.

"You're not serious. That must have been—" Teri began.

"Millions of dollars," Monique supplied. "And that's not all. Her bank accounts were totally cleaned out."

"But why?" Jennifer asked.

Monique shrugged. "Who knows? Once the bank officials realized Mary was dead, they moved to put a claim against the mansion and its furnishings. Eileen received the news by registered mail this morning.

"This whole mess is a nightmare," Monique continued. "Eileen has enough on her hands with the humiliation of being charged with a murder she didn't commit. And now she has to deal with the mess Mary made of the estate."

"When did Mary do all of this?" Jennifer asked. "She *was* the one who did it?"

"Oh, yes. Over a period beginning about eight months ago, although there were one or two fairly substantial withdrawals the year before. She left only enough to operate the household, plus a little spending money." Monique, obviously exhausted, found a spot on the couch.

She'd cashed it all in. Every dime.

Jennifer sat down on a dining chair, thoroughly confused, everything she'd thought about Mary's situation askew.

"Can the money be traced?" Leigh Ann asked.

"She took most of it in bearer bonds, so no, it can't."

"Why would she need cash like that?" Jennifer asked.

"Only one reason I can think of," Teri offered.

"Blackmail," Leigh Ann supplied.

"Right on. Someone had the goods on that old broad and was making the squeeze." Teri had been reading too much of her own writing.

"That's a leap," Jennifer argued.

"What? You're the one who told us she blackmailed her uncle. Sounds to me like someone along the line was simply returning the favor," Teri suggested.

"What uncle?" Monique asked.

"I'll explain it to you later," Jennifer promised. It was way too late to catch her up right then. "What could someone have on Mary to blackmail her?"

Leigh Ann put up her hand as though she were in school. "I've got a theory. Three people, other than Mary, died after she arrived at the Ashton mansion: Clarisse, Juliet, and Shelby. I say she killed them all."

"Leigh Ann! That's ridiculous. Clarisse was ill—" Monique insisted.

"And should have been recovering but didn't," Jennifer pointed out, thoughts tumbling through her mind. "But there's no doubt that Juliet committed suicide."

"Says who?" Teri chimed in. "Exactly whose word do we have that Juliet killed herself anyway?"

"Melba's, Luther's, the police department's," Jennifer offered.

"Right. They didn't have the forensic tools back in the Seventies that we have now," Leigh Ann said.

"It was a locked room," Jennifer reminded them.

"Always ways around that," Leigh Ann insisted.

That was true. She'd even written a locked-room mystery.

"And Shelby?" Jennifer raised an eyebrow.

"Well, maybe she didn't kill Shelby," Leigh Ann admitted. "If she were going to, surely she would have arranged an 'accident' for him when she was younger. But it makes all kinds of sense for Mary to get rid of the women in his life: Clarisse so she could marry him, and Juliet so he would focus on her. But, of course, that backfired."

Could Mary have actually killed Juliet? Somehow Jennifer doubted it. Even if her theory was wrong about why Juliet died and Mary had wanted the girl out of the way, surely she wouldn't have been so foolish as to harm her. It'd be too big a risk. If Shelby ever suspected, he would have turned her out, marriage vows or no. But Clarisse . . . that was a different matter altogether. She had everything to gain with Clarisse out of the picture.

"So who are you suggesting blackmailed her?" Jennifer asked.

"You said it yourself: Melba or Luther. They were there, in that house, all those years. They knew what was going on," Teri insisted.

"And why now?" Jennifer asked

"That one's a slam dunk," Teri said. "It wasn't until after Shelby's death that Mary actually had control of the money."

In a way, Leigh Ann's theory made a good deal of sense.

"If what you're suggesting is true, one of them recently came into a whole lot of cash." Jennifer glanced at Monique. "It might be worth checking out."

Monique nodded. "Got any suggestions as to how we might do that?"

"Isn't that illegal?" Leigh Ann threw in.

"Probably, but I know someone who could find out for us," Jennifer said.

"Who?" Monique asked.

"Johnny Zeeman."

"That sleazy private eye?" Monique wrinkled her nose, something Jennifer had never seen her do. "You know I don't approve—"

"Oh, Johnny's all right," Jennifer interrupted. Sleazy or not, he was darned good at his job, and he'd watched out for her more than once. He'd insisted she learn how to use a gun, and for that, she owed him her life. And at least a little defense when someone attacked his character.

"Then do it," Monique insisted, throwing up her hands. "You seem determined to do as you please anyway."

Jennifer shook her head. It was a fine line, this dance, trying to do what she had to without alienating Monique by threatening her leadership of their small group.

And Monique had a valid point. It was as if they were all rushing along with some weird theory, and Monique was reluctantly being pulled in their wake.

"Tell me, then," Jennifer asked Teri, "if someone was blackmailing her, why Mary was killed?"

"That makes the most sense of all," Leigh Ann answered instead. "Once the money was delivered, she was of no use to the blackmailers. Better to get rid of her than have her go to the police."

The doorbell sounded, and Jennifer looked at her watch. Cripes. It had to be Dee Dee to pick up the salads for tomorrow's parties.

As Teri leapt up to open the door, Jennifer slipped into the kitchen. She caught a quick glimpse of a flustered Dee Dee as she swept into the room.

Dee Dee was only a couple of years older than Jennifer, but life seemed so much simpler for her. She had a settled look to her that came with a husband and a routine that included chauffeuring her little girl to school and dance lessons in a minivan. She found joy in day-to-day living in a way Jennifer couldn't even imagine. Sometimes she envied her. And sometimes not.

"Hey, Teri," she heard Dee Dee say.

Quickly, she pulled a large Tupperware container of slaw from the freezer. Better to get Dee Dee in and out before she got wind of what they were discussing. She didn't need her on her case right now, hovering and worrying, and she certainly didn't have time to explain all the events of the past week—what a horrific thought—or calm her fears about what Jennifer had gotten herself into this time.

"I'll have everything out for you in less than two minutes," Jennifer called.

"Great!" Dee Dee hollered back.

"Leigh, Monique." She could hear Dee Dee greeting her friends. "What are you all doing here? Where's April? I thought your group only met on Monday nights."

"We do, but we're—" Leigh Ann began.

"Brainstorming," Jennifer yelled over her shoulder. It wasn't really a lie. It was exactly what they were doing, but darned if she wasn't going to have to watch not only what she said but also what Leigh Ann and Teri said.

Where the heck was that fruit salad? She knew she'd put it in there somewhere. Ah, there it was hiding behind the fudge ripple ice cream. She turned when the phone rang. As if she didn't have enough to juggle.

"Not to worry," Leigh Ann called out. "I've got it." She grabbed the wall phone and took it back around the corner, stretching the cord as far as it would go. "Jennifer Marsh's residence . . . uh-huh . . . no, I understand. . . . I'll be sure she gets the message. . . . I'll have her call you. . . . Really? . . . No, of course . . . Good-bye.

"You forgot your appointment at the Red Cross yesterday," Leigh Ann sang out. "But they're not mad. They'd like for you to reschedule as soon as you can. They have a special pin to give you when you come in. The woman said she clipped it to your file, and she'll mail it to you if she doesn't see you in a week."

Jennifer's hand closed on the fruit salad and she pulled it out, staring at it as though it were some foreign object.

"What are you doing in there? I thought you already had everything ready," Dee Dee called.

She dug further back under a large bag of frozen peas and drew out a second container of fruit. Then she stuffed both salads, along with the coleslaw and a container of sweet sauce she took from the refrigerator, into a grocery bag. Finally, she ducked back out from behind the kitchen partition. "Here," she said, thrusting the sack into Dee Dee's hands.

"What about the vegetable bouquets?" Dee Dee's face sagged. "That's what our clients really want. The rest of this is just . . . just food."

"I've got most of them shaped and floating in ice water. All I have to do is stick them on the green skewers, add the leaves, and put them in a vase. I'll get them to you in plenty of time, I promise. You know they don't last once they're all put together, and I'm sure you don't want to take the pieces and do it yourself."

"Okay. But don't forget," Dee Dee warned her. "You've got that crazed look you get when you're plotting your books. Are you up to something?"

She shoved Dee Dee out the door. The woman could read her way too well. "Don't worry about it. I've got a handle on it—all of it. I'll have the vegetable flowers and the vases in your hands before church in the morning."

"I go to Sunday school."

"Right. Before Sunday school."

She shut the door, turned to the group, and leaned back against it, hoping she did indeed remember to stop by Dee Dee's in the morning. "Okay, here's the deal. Somebody's come into a good bit of money, just like Leigh Ann said. I'll call Johnny and get him to find out for sure who that is. I'll ask him to check out everybody who's had anything to do with Mary in the last year, including Malcolm Reed. I want to make sure I'm right about this.

"Leigh Ann, you go down to the historical society sometime Monday and see if they've got an architectural plan for the Ashton mansion. If they don't, go to city hall and find out where such plans exist."

Monique raised both eyebrows at her. "Exactly why do you need plans of the mansion and, if you do, why not ask Eileen?"

She didn't have time for a power struggle with Monique. Monique would just have to cope with her being in charge for once. "I'd rather Eileen didn't know what we're doing, or anybody else for that matter, not yet anyway."

"Are you saying you still think she's a suspect?" Monique drew herself up, full of indignation.

"I'm not saying anything, not yet," Jennifer assured her.

"Okay, but what do I do when I get them?" Leigh Ann asked, obviously more interested in her task than what was going on between Jennifer and Monique.

"Make copies if at all possible—although how you would do that I don't know—and bring them back here.

"Teri, you check out the situation with the courts. See if anything was filed concerning Shelby's will, if he ever granted Mary a power of attorney, and if the competency suit was the only motion filed by Eileen."

"So much for lunch Monday," Teri grumbled.

"Monique," Jennifer forged ahead, "do you have any idea which travel agent Mary used?"

"Same one I do, but—"

"Great. See if Mary made any trips over the past year. Short ones, probably only for a weekend."

"Why?"

"I just want to know if she went anywhere. And if anyone went with her."

"What about April?" Leigh Ann asked. "She'll be upset if she hears you left her out."

Geez. They were all back in middle school. "I'm sure she has enough to keep her busy with her book being bought—"

"Leigh Ann's right. She'll be hurt," Teri warned.

"Okay. I'll ask her to check with Shelby's lawyer's office to see if we can find out what really happened to that will."

"And what are you going to do?" Leigh Ann asked Jennifer.

"Call Sam and get in touch with a forensic chemist."

"A chemist?" Leigh Ann stared at her as though she'd lost her mind.

"Don't worry about it," Jennifer brushed her off. "We're not going to know for sure what happened until we've found Mary's body, but I think I may know exactly how to do it."

"How?"

"I can't explain it all to you quite yet. I want all of you out of here. Now." Jennifer shooed Leigh Ann and Teri toward the door. Monique refused to be shooed, but at least she went. "And I want everyone back here Tuesday evening, no later than seven o'clock. That will give you all an extra day if you run into any problems Monday. Remember, I'm counting on you, Leigh Ann. We need those plans."

"We'll see you Monday night, right? At our writers' meeting?" Leigh Ann asked.

Jennifer shook her head. "I can't make it."

Monique's stare felt like it was boring right through her.

"But . . ." Teri began

"But what?" Jennifer asked.

"You've never missed. Not once in all the years we've been meeting."

"Sure she did," Leigh Ann reminded them. "That time she thought she had chicken pox."

"That's right. And she would have come then if April had already had them," Teri added.

"Do you mind? I'm standing right here," Jennifer reminded them.

"Yeah, we noticed." Teri lifted an eyebrow at her, and Jennifer shoved the lot of them out the door.

Monique was still having none of it. Her body language insisted she wanted an explanation now, not Tuesday night, but Jennifer couldn't help it. She couldn't risk being stopped before she even gave her theory a chance.

In the hall, Leigh Ann turned toward her, her mouth open, ready to speak, but Jennifer shut the door. She didn't have time for another word. She was already almost a week late. She just hoped she wasn't too late.

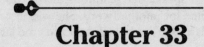

# Chapter 33

"I can't believe you got these," Jennifer marveled, as she carefully placed the original architectural drawings for the Ashton mansion on her dining table. The edges curled up as she unrolled the thick old paper, and Leigh Ann, Teri, April, and Monique each held a corner. She grabbed four books off the shelf near her desk and gave them each one to weigh down a corner.

*"Choose Your Poison,"* Leigh Ann read the title of her book out loud.

*"Insect Detectives,"* April recited hers. "Yuck. If that's the kind of research you do, I'll stick to children's books."

"Insects lay their eggs in corpses exposed to the elements, and forensic experts can tell by the stages how long—" Jennifer started.

"Okay, that's more than I ever wanted to know about bodies in the woods," Leigh Ann told her. "I have to have these plans back to the historical society by ten o'clock tomorrow morning when they open."

"I think it's amazing you managed to get them at all," Monique said.

"They have two sets," Leigh Ann explained. "I don't think they'll miss one overnight. Besides, it's not like I *stole* them."

"Yeah, right." Teri said. "I don't think they're running a lending library over there."

"How'd you do it?" April asked.

"I just put on a big smile," Leigh Ann demonstrated, "acted like I knew what I was doing, and made eye contact. That way, no one thinks you're up to something, and they're not likely to be looking at your hands. Works almost every time."

"Babies are even better," April assured her. "If I'd known what you were doing, I could have loaned you Colette. It's amazing what you can conceal in a stroller."

"Would you look at this place?" Teri said, having no more of the baby talk. "I knew it was big but this really *is* a mansion."

"Okay, Monique. You know that house better than any of us. Take a look," Jennifer insisted, stepping back out of the way.

Monique drew out her drugstore reading glasses, perched them on her nose, and scanned the plans, which covered the three main floors, the basement, and the attic. "I don't know what you want me to say."

"Does it look like you remember it?"

Monique nodded.

"And you don't see anything unusual?"

"Not a thing."

"Fine. Note that the second and third floors seem to have the exact same floor plan, with four bedrooms, two on each side of each landing."

Jennifer grabbed a calculator from a drawer in her desk and was immediately back to the table. "Let's see if the numbers add up."

As Teri read off the interior dimensions of the third floor, east to west, using Juliet's bedroom and the one next to it, Jennifer plugged them into the calculator.

"Don't forget to add at least eight or more inches for the depth of each of the walls," Monique reminded her.

"Right. I'll make it twelve."

"Okay, what's that give us?" Leigh Ann asked.

Jennifer looked back and forth from the number for the exterior dimension and the number in the calculator. "It's off by a good six feet."

"Did you remember to include the linen closet?" April asked, hovering over Jennifer's shoulder.

"Yep," Teri assured her.

"Is that storage area still there?" Monique asked.

"Yes, but they used part of it to make a bathroom," Jennifer assured her.

"Well of course there's unaccounted space," Monique insisted. "The fireplaces are inset into those interior walls."

They exchanged looks across the table. "Let's try the bedrooms on the other side of the landing," Jennifer suggested. "They're proportioned a little differently, but . . ."

This time April read the numbers as Jennifer plugged them into the calculator. "See? The dimensions listed account for all but three feet of the space, and they share fireplaces on the interior walls, just like the rooms across the landing do.

"You don't need that much extra space to build fireplaces. That's where the passages lie," Jennifer announced, "between the interior walls of the bedrooms on that side of the house."

"But why don't they appear on the plans?" Leigh Ann asked.

"Because these are the official drawings," Jennifer explained.

She turned to Monique. "Do you think Eileen knows about the passages?"

Monique stared at her, not even trying to hide her disapproval. "You're making a major leap. Who's to say how accurate these plans are anyway?"

Jennifer returned the stare. She realized she was usurping what Monique considered her God-given authority and invading her family turf in a way she had no right to, but she had no choice. "Maybe they aren't accurate. But if they are, how obvious do you think it would be that those walls are especially thick?"

Monique shook her head. "Those rooms are really large. I'm not sure you would notice. You'd have to be looking for it."

Jennifer scanned the plans again. "And look below, on the first floor." She tapped her finger on the paper. "There seems to be a series of storage areas like closets. Six to one that that last one doesn't open out anywhere."

"And there's a similar area in the basement," Teri pointed out.

"Not to sound stupid, but why do we care?" Leigh Ann asked.

"It's how they got the body out," Teri explained, "without having to take it down the stairs."

"It's how they got onto the third floor without passing me to pick up the block," Jennifer added.

"Wouldn't that be risky?" April asked. "Surely the murderer wouldn't come right up into the room you were in."

"Not into Juliet's room, into the room adjoining. That way they could slip into the hall and come around to my door. I suspect there are openings into all the bedrooms on that side of the house."

"Hold on," Monique butted in. "You're letting your imaginations run away with you—all of you. You write fiction, remember? What works in your books doesn't necessarily work in real life."

"Juliet got in and out of that house pretty much at will without her parents knowing it, Eileen as good as told me that. We know Mary sometimes locked her in her room. So you tell me how she did it if not through some passageway. I wouldn't be at all surprised if Malcolm Reed didn't slip in and out as well. As a matter of fact, that might have been the easiest way. He could even spend the night, and Shelby and Mary would never know it. I bet Malcolm loved that. If they knocked on her door to check on Juliet, there'd she be."

Monique just stared at her. She obviously didn't believe a word of it.

"Why did they come back to pick up the block anyway?" Leigh Ann asked, bravely ignoring Monique.

"They didn't, exactly. They came to make sure I could get out. They wanted me to find the murder scene and to call the police," Jennifer explained. "But not before they were ready for me to do it."

"But you were already loose," Monique pointed out, leaning further over the plans and studying them. At least she was listening and not rejecting Jennifer's theory out of hand.

"They didn't know that," Jennifer said relieved. She needed Monique's help. She couldn't go on to the next step without her. "And they didn't count on me calling the police on my cell phone."

"So they picked up the block . . ." Teri began.

"In hopes I hadn't realized that was why I couldn't get the door open. Or that I'd forget or think I was confused when it disappeared. They didn't know I had a flashlight and had seen it under the door."

"Wouldn't that be risky?" April asked.

"Not necessarily. They knew I'd be focused on what was going on below and it was really dark. I never would have looked behind that door. I might have even forgotten about it if Nicholls hadn't had such a nose for detail. He's the one who sent someone looking for it."

"Someone else might forget, but not you," Leigh Ann insisted.

"These passages are all just theory," Monique stated.

"No, they aren't. Leigh Ann and Teri gave us evidence they exist."

"When?" they asked in unison.

"When you told me the neighbor said that Amy Loggins escaped from the house. She must have somehow discovered a way into the passage, probably tripped it by accident, and slipped through, but she was so confused, she must not have known exactly where she was. She certainly didn't seem to be able to find her way back."

"Where do you think it comes out?" Teri asked.

"Somewhere on the property. It shouldn't be all that difficult to find. The lot isn't all that huge."

"Do you think there's evidence in the passageways?" Leigh Ann asked.

"I'd be surprised if there wasn't. It must be dark as night in there, and you can bet they're not wired with electric lights. If there is a blood trail, that's where it is. We know the police didn't find one down the main staircase."

"So why are we looking at these?" April asked. "Why not just tell the police about them?"

"I don't want to suggest the police go searching for something I'm not absolutely certain they'll find. At the moment, my credibility is tenuous at best."

"Why?" Teri seemed totally confused.

"Let's just say, I've presented them with some thoughts to consider. I don't want any missteps, any more reasons for them to believe I'm the looney mystery writer they may already think I am. What'd you find out at the courthouse?"

"Mary did have power of attorney, starting about two years ago after Shelby got really ill with heart disease," Teri told them.

"So he trusted her enough for that. Maybe he did let Mary see his will."

"Shelby, for all his good heart, was not a very forthright man," Monique told them.

"Old school, huh? Well, he was kidding himself if he thought he could keep anything from Mary," Leigh Ann threw in.

"Exactly," Jennifer agreed. "If he kept a copy of the will in the house, hidden or otherwise, I'm sure she wouldn't rest until she found it."

"Do you actually think she destroyed that will?" Leigh Ann asked.

Jennifer shrugged. "Why not? She lived with the man for over forty years. I suspect she felt she'd earned that house and everything that went with it. With the animosity that existed between her and Eileen, I wouldn't be surprised if she expected to be turned out into the street."

"Eileen would never do that," Monique insisted.

"I'm sure you're right, but Mary would have done it to Eileen, and that made it plausible to her. She had to get the estate settled in her favor. With Shelby dying intestate, the entire fortune went to her since Juliet was already dead."

"April, did you get hold of David Lambert's legal secretary?"

"Finally. Next time you pass out jobs, I'd like to be present. I had the devil of a time finding her. She admitted it was possible that someone had picked up Mr. Ashton's will the week that Lambert died. She wasn't sure what procedure she was to follow, but she said she would have insisted on a request signed by Mr. Ashton.

She conceded she wouldn't have thought to check his signature against the one in the files."

It was all making sense to her. More and more sense.

"What did you find out from your travel agent?" Jennifer asked Monique.

"You were right. Mary made three weekend hops to the Bahamas during the past six months."

"Okay. That's what I needed to know."

"What about that detective friend of yours?" Monique asked.

"He discovered a substantial deposit made to an account about ten days ago, nothing suspiciously large, about $10,000. The rest must be somewhere else."

"You mean 'else' as in buried in the backyard or in the mattress stuffing?" Leigh Ann asked.

"I mean 'else' as in an offshore account."

"You knew which account it was before you asked Johnny to find out, didn't you?" Teri asked.

"I had my suspicions, but we can't give that information to the police. They'll have to come up with it on their own."

"Who are you talking about?" Leigh Ann was about to burst at the seams.

"Depositing money into one's own bank account is not a crime," Jennifer reminded her. "I'm not about to accuse anybody of anything, not in front of you or anyone else, not until we've got the evidence we need."

"You're no fun," Leigh Ann pouted.

"Sure she is." April grinned. "Beats bath time at my house. Craig should be mopping up the floor right about now."

"So how exactly do you plan to get this evidence?" Teri asked.

"I think it's time the five of us did a little exploring."

"Oh, Lord. You couldn't possibly mean . . ." Leigh Ann began.

"We'll get shot for trespassing," Teri said.

"Not if we've got permission," Jennifer told them. She turned to Monique. "I want you to call Eileen and get us access to the Ashton mansion, all parts of it, inside and out."

"What do you want me to tell her?"

"Tell her we want to find evidence of her innocence."

"When do you want to go?"

"Tomorrow night. Say about eight o'clock."

"Heck. That's really close to sunset," Teri pointed out.

"And it's my kids' bedtime," April said.

Jennifer smiled. "Actually, I don't want Melba—or anybody else for that matter—to know what we're up to. Wear jeans and bring gloves and flashlights."

"What for?" Leigh Ann asked.

"I can't ask the police to believe me when the four of you still have some doubts. We're going to find out how they did it. We're going to find those passageways."

# Chapter 34

"It's almost eight-thirty. Where *is* Monique?" Leigh Ann hopped nervously back and forth on the balls of her feet. "If she doesn't show her face in five minutes, I say we all go home."

"Keep it down," Teri ordered. "She'll be here."

"It's bad enough that April backed out," Leigh Ann added. "Little Colette with a fever. Hah! She just doesn't want to have to explain to Craig when she gets herself arrested for trespassing."

Jennifer shushed them both and took another look around the back of the mansion. The light was dimming fast. If Monique didn't get there soon, they could give up all hope of finding the entrance that night.

During the half hour they'd waited, they had discreetly scouted the property. The last thing they needed was to arouse some nosy neighbor's suspicions. And they hadn't touched anything. They wouldn't. Leigh Ann was right. They shouldn't be there, not until they had Eileen's permission.

They'd checked for disturbances around the foundation, but none were visible. They'd also walked around the outbuildings. Both were padlocked from the outside. It'd be unlikely that the opening would be inside one of them. Too easy to get trapped. No, it had to be somewhere else, but where?

Behind the house, steps led down ivy-covered banks to a formal rose garden with stone benches and two small fountains. Near the driveway they'd found a storm drain. Nowhere had they found a good place for an entrance, but then Jennifer hadn't expected they would.

Two figures walked past the side of the house. For a moment, her heart caught in her throat. Then she recognized Eileen and Monique. "You didn't have to—"

"This I want to see for myself," Eileen said. She nodded at both Leigh Ann and Teri. Formal introductions hardly seemed necessary under the circumstances. She, too, was dressed in jeans. Jennifer would have sworn she didn't own a pair.

"I couldn't convince her to stay home," Monique explained.

"Fine," Jennifer agreed. "If it were my freedom on the line, I'd insist on being here, too."

"So where do we start?" Eileen asked.

"I think we should split up," Jennifer said. "We're looking for something stone or concrete, possibly metal. It may be covered with dirt or vegetation, and you can bet it will be well hidden. If it weren't, you would have found it when you were playing out here as a child."

Eileen nodded.

"Leigh Ann and Teri, you two check once more around the foundation of the house and the outbuildings. Monique and Eileen, why don't you look down through the garden, and I'll check that drain."

They fanned out, with Teri ducking through the shrubbery and walking against the house, while Leigh Ann followed on the outside and offered suggestions that Teri ignored. Jennifer approached the grate of the drain just as Monique and Eileen headed down the steps toward the garden.

The drain looked to be exactly what it was, with a

drop that would make it difficult to climb out of. Jennifer got down on her hands and knees and pulled, but the heavy metal shielding the hole wouldn't budge. No way could someone as small as Juliet have moved it by herself. Abandoning it, she checked the stone patio at the back door by tugging at each block, but they all appeared to be cemented in place. If there had once been an opening there, it was now inaccessible.

A whistle startled her, and she turned to see Monique waving her flashlight in the air. She ran to her immediately, and Leigh Ann and Teri came up beside her at the steps down to the garden. Eileen was standing there, holding back a thick weave of ivy. Exposed on the side of the steps was a metal plate. When Monique kicked it with her shoe, it gave off a hollow sound.

"It moves," she said, pulling it back on rusted hinges.

A narrow entrance gaped at them.

Jennifer, Leigh Ann, and Teri cast their beams downward, illuminating stone steps leading into the darkness. On the second step, against one wall, sat an old-fashioned lantern. But something else made Jennifer's heart race even faster. She dropped down on one knee, letting the beam from her light shine full force on the steps. Directing her light from step to step, she could see dark round drops, dark red drops of blood.

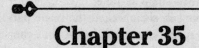

# Chapter 35

The breath nearly left Jennifer's body. She stared at the gaping hole leading down into the earth, caught in that strange unreality where theory becomes fact, theory she couldn't quite believe herself. Until she saw the blood.

"Either do it or don't," she heard Teri say from behind her.

"I'm not at all sure you should go down there," Monique warned.

"From what I know of Jennifer," Eileen said, "I doubt we could keep her out. We'll wait for you here. If you're not back in five minutes, we'll go around to the house."

Jennifer took a deep breath, stood, and plunged forward. If she waited to think about it, she'd never have the courage to go in.

"We shouldn't be doing this," Jennifer told Leigh Ann and Teri, who crowded behind her. "Whatever you do, don't step on any of the blood. Nicholls is going to have my head as it is."

Carefully, using the stone walls as support and stepping as far to the sides as possible, Jennifer lowered herself down the narrow steps, her two friends scrambling after her. When the stairs stopped, they could no longer see the blood.

Now they were in a long underground passage built more than a century and a half ago, the roof so low they had to bend to avoid hitting their heads and the width so narrow they had to proceed single file. It was like entering another world, one that Jennifer wasn't at all sure she wanted to be in.

The air was cooler, but stagnant, musty, smelling of the earth all around them. Their feet hit against hard-packed dirt, almost like stone. Flashes from their lights revealed supports running along the top and bottom and bracing the sides, overhead beams defying the earth to push its way into this carefully hollowed-out tunnel. Without flashlights, it would have been darker than night.

Poor Amy, lost in that blackness, confused and terrified, like some poor soul in a Poe story. She could almost hear her sobs.

And Juliet and Malcolm. She could almost hear their laughter as they played their youthful game of hide-and-seek. They would have stopped for a quick kiss, or more, before they tumbled out from under the steps, out into the freedom of the night and away from her parents' watchful eyes.

A hand on Jennifer's shoulder made her jump. "It's like we've stepped out of the world," Leigh Ann whispered.

"More like into a tomb," Teri offered from behind.

This death imagery was not particularly helpful. Jennifer took Leigh Ann's hand. "Get hold of Teri, too," she told her. Then she moved forward, too fascinated to go back and too terrified to let herself think about where they actually were. She wished she had a lantern, but she hadn't dared to touch the one on the steps. A lantern would offer less directed light and let them see what it was really like down there—not that the ability to see would necessarily be comforting.

"You didn't buy all that about Eileen not knowing

about this tunnel, did you?" Teri's voice sounded strangely distant, dampened by the earth around them.

Jennifer stopped and turned. "Why not?" The beam from her flashlight cast an eerie glow past Leigh Ann and across Teri's dark features.

"If she killed Mary—and, by the way, she gets my vote—we can't believe a word she says. She could have knocked Monique over the head by now and be sealing up the entrance this very moment. I read this book once—"

Leigh Ann let go of Jennifer and grabbed the throat of Teri's T-shirt. "Don't even think about discussing that down here," she warned. "If you want to keep me calm, you'll keep moving. I suffer from claustrophobia, and it's feeling a little cramped in here about now."

"It would have been nice if you'd told us about your phobia *before* we went down the rabbit hole," Jennifer said.

"Me? She's the one turning this into the Cask of Amontillado, suggesting we're going to be walled up in this godforsaken pit in the ground, clawing at each other for the last bit of breath before we—"

Jennifer clamped a hand over Leigh Ann's mouth. "Not another word. Either of you." Writers. And to think she was one of them.

Jennifer turned back around. They were a good ways in, but the tunnel stretched forward for what looked like forever. She'd estimated only thirty feet, but that was just to the foundation of the house. If the tunnel came out where she suspected, between where the bedrooms should be on the upper floors, it stretched farther still, about halfway down the side of the house.

They moved forward as quickly as they could, not daring to speak another word. She could only hope their courage would outlast the distance.

A solid wall of dirt loomed in front of them, and she stopped dead, Leigh Ann bumping into her from behind. A brief sweat of panic washed over Jennifer. Leigh Ann wasn't the only one on the edge of a claustrophobic fit.

"What's wrong?" she heard Teri ask.

"Nothing," she assured her, flashing her light to the right.

Thank God. A small opening. Filling it was a framed-in wooden platform. They must be at the house.

Jennifer shone her light upward. It was immediately joined by the beams from Teri and Leigh Ann's lights. The shaft seemed to go up forever, at least four floors. They could see some of the interior structure of the walls.

"Why'd they have to make this house so darn tall?" Leigh Ann asked. "And what the heck is that thing?" Her light outlined the platform, flecks of dark red here and there.

"It's a dumbwaiter," Teri said.

"Not exactly," Jennifer corrected, stepping onto it. "More like an open elevator."

"You're not getting me on that thing," Leigh Ann declared.

"No one's asking you to go," Jennifer assured her, tugging against the frame. It seemed solid enough. A switch was attached to one of the wooden supports. She flipped it and the platform started to move upward. She grabbed at one side and hastily flipped it off. The elevator shuddered to a stop about a foot off the ground. She pushed a lever, and when she flipped the switch once more, it moved back down.

"Electric motor," Teri pointed out, "a quiet one at that."

"Obviously not original," Jennifer observed. "I'll bet the first one was muscle-powered with ropes and pulleys."

"Who cares?" Leigh Ann sighed. "I just want to go home."

"Okay," Jennifer told them, "there are two ways out of here: back the way we came or up."

"That's a choice?" Leigh Ann asked, close to tears.

"Up is faster," Teri declared, stepping aboard, "and less closed in."

"Did I mention I'm afraid of heights, too?" Leigh Ann added.

So was Jennifer, but up got her vote. She hadn't come that far to go back now, and, at least in the dark, they wouldn't see how far down they could fall.

"Come on." Teri offered Leigh Ann a hand onto the platform.

"It doesn't have any sides on it," she wailed.

"Right. Ralph Nader hadn't been born when it was built," Teri pointed out.

Leigh Ann curled up in the middle. "They'll find us if we die in here, won't they?"

"Yep," Jennifer assured her. "They'll even pull our bodies out for a decent burial."

"Not if Eileen—" Teri began.

"Teri," Jennifer warned.

"What?"

"If you get her started, I'm leaving you both in the tunnel."

"No more about . . . you know," Teri promised. She held out her hand to take Jennifer's light, freeing her to operate the controls. They swung upward in a surprisingly free and easy ride. Only a quiet whir could be heard.

"Amazing," Teri noted. "How high do we go?"

"All the way," Jennifer told her as she heard Leigh Ann groan.

When they stopped on the third floor, they could easily

see the frames for the fireplaces. The flues from below came up through the platform between the walls and joined with the flues on that floor. Then they headed up through the attic and, no doubt, on through the roof.

Jennifer took back her light, stepped off, and offered a hand to Teri. They both helped Leigh Ann up to find her way onto more solid ground.

"Geez. You'd think someone would clean around here once in a while," Leigh Ann griped.

"Secret passages," Teri reminded her. "Secret as in nobody knows they're here. You can't exactly send the maid in to do a little tidying up."

Indeed dust was everywhere, sitting inches thick on the studs and on the sides of the flooring. It made Jennifer cringe wondering what insect life thrived there. But the center of the boards showed evidence that someone had moved through there not all that long ago. The dust was thinner where something had scuffed it aside.

"This is truly creepy," Leigh Ann declared, flashing her light over a huge spider web and getting as close to Jennifer as possible. "Ugh. What is crawling on me?" She swatted at her neck.

"Nothing," Teri insisted, flashing her light over Leigh Ann and then directing it at the fireplace. "Look there."

A burlap sack was pushed against the far wall. Jennifer bent down and shook off the dust. Bad idea. It caught in her throat and, for a moment, she choked on it. Thankful for her gloves, she opened the bag and shone her light inside. There appeared to be a stack of papers, some candles, and several books. One was larger than the others. It looked like a ledger. She pulled it out and carefully opened it. Written in faded ink were apparently the minutes from some sort of meetings. George Washington Ashton must indeed have held secret gatherings.

Names, dates, and times were also listed. Members must have used the passage to come and go unseen.

She reached back into the sack and retrieved a paper from the stack. Letters printed in an old style called for the South to break from the North. It crumbled in her hand.

"If someone was in and out of these tunnels, why was that sack never brought out?" Leigh Ann asked over her shoulder.

"If it had been," Jennifer said, marveling over what she was holding, "whoever produced it would have to tell where they got it. Better to leave it here and keep the passages their secret."

"I found it," Teri called out. Almost immediately, a portion of the wall swung out and straight into Juliet's room. Teri disappeared after it and then came right back. "The trip is concealed in the molding. It's completely hidden from the other side."

"They'll be worried about us," Leigh Ann suggested. "That is, assuming Monique isn't dead and Eileen isn't planning our deaths."

Jennifer nodded. She'd had more than enough dark and cramped spaces to last her for some time. She returned the old volume to the sack and left it in place. She had one more thing she had to do.

"I really don't feel well." Leigh Ann again, only this time she put a hand over her mouth.

"Okay, let's get you out of here," Jennifer said. "Teri, take her into Juliet's room."

"But there's a ghost in there," Leigh Ann whined.

"Choose your poison: ghost or tunnel. I have no intentions of going back underground," Jennifer assured her.

"Besides, I figure a ghost can glide right into that tunnel every bit as easily as she can into that room," Teri pointed out. "They do pass through walls, don't they?"

"Just move it," Jennifer ordered. She climbed back onto the platform, threw the switch, and it began to descend back into the pit.

"Where are you going?" Leigh Ann called frantically. "I thought you weren't going back out that way."

"I'm not." She hit the switch and the elevator jerked to an abrupt stop one floor down. Two more voices had joined Leigh Ann's and Teri's above her. Good. Monique and Eileen had come around and into the house. Just in time to help Teri calm down Leigh Ann.

Reluctantly, she flashed her light across the landing. She had to know if there was an opening into Mary's room. At first the area seemed clear, but then the beam caught something shoved back between the two fireplaces. It was a thick roll with fringe dangling from the coiled edge, covered with telltale dark splotches. The rug from Mary's bedroom.

She put a hand over her nose and mouth. A putrid odor wafted in her direction.

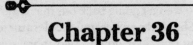

# Chapter 36

Now that she knew exactly what had happened to Mary, she had to prove it. And Luther, whether he liked it or not, was going to have to play a part.

"I understand how you feel," Jennifer insisted, perched on the same slipcovered chair she'd fought with exactly one week ago.

"Oh, I doubt that." Luther puffed on his pipe and looked most disapprovingly at her. He sat in the recliner he'd been in when she visited him. It gave the illusion that he hadn't moved since.

He was irritated, not just with the questions she was asking, but also because she'd interrupted the televangelist's sermon he'd been watching. He turned the TV down low, but she could still hear the amens that rang up from the studio audience. He stared past her with a deep frown between his eyes.

"Most inappropriate having someone who works for you meddling in your personal affairs," he said. "When you work in a private home it becomes a delicate balance, but you wouldn't know that, would you, girl?" He looked her dead in the eye.

Again, smoke puffed around the pipe stem in silent rebuke.

She was trying to be patient, really she was. "I'm not asking you to betray a confidence. I simply asked if Mr.

Ashton would have had reason to hide his will from Mary instead of destroying it like she said he did, and where he might have hid it if he did."

"I heard you. It's not the question that's at issue here. It's whether or not I'm gonna choose to answer it. Just what business is it of yours anyhow?"

"Mary Ashton made it my business. She hired me to find out who was plotting murder against her. If she were still with us, I might have had to learn about that delicate balance you're talking about, but she's not. I realize you weren't in the Ashtons' employ when Mr. Ashton died, but you must have been working there when he revised his will. Surely, he did it after Juliet died, and probably at least once more since then."

He nodded, still studying her.

"Did he let Mary see it?" she asked.

"You say my talking to you will help set everything right?"

"Yes," she assured him.

"Well, Mr. Shelby certainly wouldn't have advertised it to Miss Mary. I suspect she wouldn't have cared much for what was in it. But no one in that house could keep secrets from that woman."

Finally an answer. So Luther did know about the will.

"You know Mary testified in court that she watched him destroy it."

"That's what I heard."

"And that's how she came to be in control of the estate. Because he died intestate."

"It was my understanding she was making all that right with her own will. Did I hear that Miss Eileen was her beneficiary?"

"Yes, which is precisely part of the trouble."

Again he nodded and puffed on his pipe. "That might not look too good for her."

"No, it doesn't, but that's not why I'm here. There were two copies of Shelby's will, one at the lawyer's office and one at home. We know the one at the lawyer's office disappeared sometime after Mr. Lambert's death and while Shelby was ill. No one at the office seems to remember sending it over to the house, but apparently everything was in a state of confusion. Mr. Lambert died unexpectedly of a heart attack and he was in practice by himself."

"He'd left me some money," Luther said, staring off. "Me and Melba both. He told me. Wasn't much, but it was something."

*Wasn't much* could mean a lot to someone like Luther.

"If Shelby did have a copy at home, where might he put it if he didn't want Mary to see it? Is there someplace, maybe in his desk, someplace she might not have found it?"

"Now what good would that do, puttin' it in some desk? That's the first place Miss Mary would look, and she wouldn't be above taking it apart piece by piece to find something if she wanted it bad. No. Don't go lookin' at the desk. I'd say try in the study, but not at the desk. And probably not in any of the furniture."

"You mean the woodwork? The walls themselves?"

"I don't know nothin'. You asked my opinion and I told it to you. What you infer is your own business. Why is this so important, now that they're both dead, Mr. Shelby and Miss Mary?"

"You're going to have to trust me on this one, Luther."

"I've lived long enough to know not to trust anyone unless I have to."

He was a sly old fox.

"Eileen's moved into the house," she told him.

One of his eyebrows rose. "So she's been released."

"Of course, days ago. On bond. She's got the best lawyers in the state."

"But why take herself back to that place, especially now?"

"She doesn't want to leave the house unoccupied. She's taken the master bedroom as her own."

He took the pipe from his mouth and leaned forward. "Where Miss Mary died?"

"Yep."

He shook his head. "Mmmmm, mmmmm! She's got seven other bedrooms to choose from and she can't find another that suits her? Couldn't pay me to do that. You don't go messin' where dark things happen, not unless you have to. It's not good for your spirit. Don't need no ghosts to tell you that."

No, she didn't.

"There's an odor in that room," she said. "Eileen's having an architect come in Monday to check it out, find the source."

"You'd think she'd have enough sense to leave well enough alone."

"Have you seen Arthur lately?" Jennifer asked.

"Oh, he comes round 'bout once a week. I expect him by tomorrow."

"Is he doing okay?"

"Seems to be."

"Has he started his business back up? I know Eileen said he could use the kitchen at the mansion. He should call her."

"Nope. He's done with all that."

"So what's he doing?"

"He calls it considering his options. That boy should never have left the Air Force. I told him that when he done it, but he don't listen to no one but himself. He wanted to cook."

"Like you."

He gave her another look. "I didn't have so many choices when I was coming up."

Point taken.

"You give him my regards when you see him, and tell him if he's interested, that Mrs. McEvoy might be looking for someone to work for her, at least while she stays at the estate."

He nodded and turned the TV back up. She let herself out.

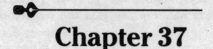

# Chapter 37

McEVOY CLEARED IN ASHTON MURDER
*by Samuel Culpepper*

*Charges against Eileen Ashton McEvoy, in the death of Mary Bedford Ashton, have been dropped for lack of evidence. In a press conference held yesterday morning, the District Attorney's office assured the public that the search for Mrs. Ashton's murderer will continue, but in other directions.*

*A knife found in the McEvoy garden cannot be positively identified as the murder weapon, even though blood and hair on the knife match that which was found at the murder scene. The absence of fingerprints on the knife casts even more doubt on Mrs. McEvoy's involvement in her sister-in-law's death.*

*In an interview, Mrs. McEvoy told this reporter, "Mary Ashton's passing has restored control of the Ashton mansion to the proper individuals. Fortunately, the substantial life insurance policy my brother Shelby took out against his wife's death and later transferred to me just prior to his passing did more than repay any debts incurred by the second Mrs. Ashton. It will close a chapter of Ashton history best forgotten. The historical society is planning a gala celebration to be held this fall at the mansion to commemorate its return to the family. Restorations are expected to begin Monday, starting with the master bedroom on the second floor."*

*When asked about her personal feelings, Mrs. McEvoy stated, "I'm just glad this whole ordeal is over."*

"Looks like you got it all in there," Jennifer told Sam.

"Just doing what I was told."

"Well, if anything will do it, I suspect this will. How many copies did you have printed?"

"Five. Nicholls has one, my editor has one, I've got this one, and the other two got doorstep delivery this morning as though they were the regular edition of the *Telegraph*."

"And the district attorney didn't have any trouble with it?"

"After what his forensic guys found? No way. He wasn't nearly as tough a sell as my editor."

"That doesn't surprise me. After all, it's his paper on the line."

"It's not as if we printed a bogus article and distributed it to the entire population of Macon."

"Right. So now all we do is sit back and watch what happens."

He nodded. "Closely."

"Closely," she agreed.

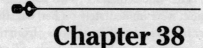

# Chapter 38

The faintest light, cast by the half moon, spread beneath each window where blood had pooled less than two weeks before. The air still held a chill and the eerie feel that this was a place where people not only lived but died.

Outlined by moonlight and shadow, a form lay still in the four-poster bed as though heavy in sleep, covered in sheet and spread, facing the carved patterns on the fireplace wall. The time: barely three A.M., in what seemed like an endless night.

Out of the darkness, a ghostly shape appeared at the wall, silhouetted in the glow of an old-fashioned lantern.

How must it look through the window to a chance passerby? As though Amy Loggins had returned one more time to announce one final victim?

The lantern found a place on the floor, and the form glided silently toward the bed, the softest glint of metal flashing in the moonlight.

And then an unearthly screech of rage filled the room as the figure lunged at the form on the bed, tearing at it, driving metal hard with each rise and thrust of the arm, each grunt of primitive fury.

Instantly light flooded the room from every corner, exposing the figure as a woman. She seemed confused, her eyes blinking against the brightness. Dressed in black from her neck to her gloved hands to her athletic shoes, she held the knife double-fisted high above her head as though to deliver one final death blow.

"What the hell?" she demanded. Two policemen, also dressed in black, were immediately on her, wrestling the knife from her hands and pulling her away from the bed. She offered no resistence, only a grim look of horror on her aging face as she looked down at a form sewn in muslin and stuffed with batting and realized that there was no blood. Puffs of down floated in the air where the knife had torn into the pillow.

"Welcome home, Mary," Jennifer said from across the room. She stared at the less-than-cultured turn of Mary's mouth and wondered how she could have ever thought her attractive. "Glad you could make it. We were about to think you weren't going to show."

She stood between Sam and Eileen McEvoy. Lieutenant Nicholls was on the other side of Eileen.

Mary squinted in their direction. "Eileen? Is that you?"

The first officer tugged Mary toward the door, slightly loosening his grip. Suddenly she ducked and lunged straight at Eileen, hatred so powerful it was almost palpable. "She murdered me!" she shrieked.

Nicholls dove for Eileen, pushing her up against the wall, his body covering hers. Two officers were immediately on top of Mary, but she'd come within a yard of them. They pulled her away.

"Arrest her," Mary demanded, full of outrage. "She snuck into this very room and slashed me to death. My blood was everywhere. You must have seen it. All that blood. All my blood." She continued to seethe, her gaze darting about the room, her eyes wild.

Then looking up at the officer, almost twice her size,

who was holding her arm, she calmed. She seemed to relax and allowed him to direct her toward the door.

Suddenly she smiled. "Oh, goodness me. I had no idea I'd have guests. I'll ring for Arthur to bring us all up some tea. You do like tea, don't you, young man?"

"Yeah, yeah, yeah," Nicholls said. "Just take her downstairs, don't talk to her, and don't question her."

She glanced back at the four of them standing there. "Really, young man, wouldn't you care for a bite to eat? I hardly feel right having all these guests in my home and not offering at least some form of refreshment. Perhaps you'd prefer coffee or . . ."

Her voice trailed off as they made their way down the grand staircase.

Eileen stood stoic, not uttering a word. But she was shaken down to her bones, Jennifer could tell. It was her eyes, once again, that betrayed.

"Aren't you going to read Mary her rights?" Jennifer asked.

"I told them not to question her. She obviously had her whole defense mapped out after one glance around that room. Sharp old broad. The fact that her competency was questioned before will play right into her defense. Bet you she'll claim to have been on vacation and have no idea what all the fuss is about."

Eileen studied Jennifer. "Don't let her fool you, you of all people."

Jennifer nodded, her heart still pounding. Only she wasn't so sure Nicholls and Eileen were right. Mary might well have slipped right over the edge and plunged into madness.

In any case, the woman wasn't likely to ever see the inside of a jail cell, not if she could make Jennifer, who knew what she was capable of, doubt her sanity. All she needed was one member of a jury. She might even be able to convince the district attorney that she was totally nuts.

They would try her on attempted murder. If Eileen McEvoy had been in that bed, and no one had been there to stop her, Mary would have killed her. She had destroyed her husband's will, stolen her husband's fortune, or more accurately, her husband's family's fortune, and she had tried to frame her sister-in-law for a murder that had never actually happened.

"So you don't think the D.A. will pursue the possibility that Mary murdered Clarisse?" Sam asked.

"I doubt it," Nicholls said. "We have enough on her to keep her busy for a good long time. If she lives to see the sunshine, I doubt she'll be a threat to anyone by the time they turn her out."

"She'll be a threat until she draws her last breath," Eileen assured him.

Jennifer was inclined to agree, sane or not.

"Besides," Nicholls added, "even if we exhume the first Mrs. Ashton's body, assuming we could talk Mrs. McEvoy here into giving us permission, what good would it do? So we find arsenic or some other poison in Clarisse Ashton's body, like Jennifer suggested, we couldn't link Mary to her death, not after all these years, not without a confession. And if the old broad was smart enough to use something that dissipates over time, we wouldn't even have that much."

"I won't let you dig her up," Eileen told him. "You'll have to have it court ordered if at all. Clarisse deserves her peace."

The four of them made their way out of the room and down the stairs of that majestic old house. "I'll need at least one more statement from each of you," Nicholls told Jennifer and Eileen. "And one from you," he added to Sam, "as to what you witnessed tonight."

Outside, two police cars had been brought around, lights flashing.

"The colors are quite delightful twirling around like that," Mrs. Ashton was saying, as they came down the front steps. Her hands were cuffed behind her back.

When she looked up, she caught Jennifer's eye. "Oh, my dear child, so nice to see you. You are staying with us, aren't you, now that I'm back? I'm so sorry you couldn't join us on holiday. We've missed you, Juliet. We've all missed you." The officer opened the back door of the car and then gently nudged her into the car, placing his hand over her forehead to protect it. The door shut and she stared up at Jennifer, smiling enigmatically.

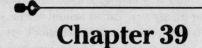

# Chapter 39

"I'm impressed," Nicholls told Jennifer, as the police car with Mary in it drove away. "You stuck with this one."

"I wouldn't have if she hadn't . . ." Jennifer confessed. Watching the car go, she wondered exactly what was going on in that woman's mind.

"What's that?" Nicholls asked.

"Mary Ashton made a mistake," Sam said. "She should never have made Jennifer promise."

"Promise what?" Eileen asked.

"That she wouldn't let her murderer get away with it."

Sam was right. If she hadn't, Jennifer would have walked away and left it all to the police. And Eileen McEvoy would be facing a charge of first-degree murder.

"But how did you know?" Nicholls asked. "What tipped you to how she did it?"

She couldn't actually tell him. She didn't really understand it herself, so how could he? It was the thing that made her plots come together when she was writing, that subconscious working of her mind that sometimes woke her from a deep sleep. How could she explain that magic moment when all the elements that played through her mind somehow finally made sense?

At least she could try.

"When I first met her," Jennifer began, "Mary seemed

resigned to dying. But even as she was telling me this, she was playing me. As I learned more about her after her 'death,' it hardly seemed logical that this manipulating woman would sit back and allow herself to be murdered."

"People are murdered all the time and how strong their personalities are doesn't save them," Nicholls told her.

"Oh, I realize that, but it was what first got me wondering, especially after I met Mrs. McEvoy. She seemed to have too much of a sense of fair play to resort to bloodshed."

"Sure, but what I was asking—" Nicholls began.

"Was how I figured out where she got all that blood to drown her bed and still walk away from it alive. It was the frozen salads I made for Dee Dee and the fact that I'd missed my appointment to give blood. And the timing, every six weeks. And Arthur's being a med tech in the Air Force, of course."

"Does she always talk like this?" Nicholls asked.

"You mean sort of in a stream-of-conscious mishmash?" Sam asked.

Nicholls nodded.

"Only when she's trying to describe her thought processes. Some wonders are best left unexplained."

"Okay then, you two," Jennifer grumped. "Plain English it is. I had my hand in the freezer and Leigh Ann was talking on the phone about missing my appointment to give blood. Then I moved the frozen peas to get to the coleslaw—"

"I didn't think you could freeze coleslaw," Eileen said.

"That's just it. You can freeze almost anything. That's what went through my mind, and I suddenly thought *what if*. What if Mary had frozen her blood? What if Arthur, the former med tech, had taken a pint from her arm just like they do at the Red Cross every six weeks or so, maybe even more often than that, over the eight months since the competency hearing? What if she'd thawed that blood, and what if the night of her 'murder,' she'd poured all of it over her bed? What if she wasn't dead at all?

"That's when I called Lieutenant Nicholls and asked him to have a forensic chemist examine a sample of the blood under a microscope to see if he could find evidence that it had been frozen."

"And did he?" Eileen asked Nicholls.

"Some of the cells showed alterations consistent with freezing. It at least raised the possibility."

"It took finding the passageways and the rug with the empty blood bags wrapped inside to get him to agree to bait Mary," Jennifer explained.

"I would never have gone along with Jennifer's screwy plan—" Nicholls began.

"Screwy?" Jennifer demanded.

"Aw c'mon. You can't tell me this plan wasn't something right out of a mystery novel."

"It wasn't," Jennifer insisted. "If it had been, Eileen would have been in that bed instead of a dummy—"

"I hardly think so," Eileen interjected.

"And we would have barely saved her at the last minute," Jennifer finished with a grin.

"But why did they leave the rug behind?" Sam asked.

"They hadn't planned to, I'm sure, but they didn't count on my phoning the police from my room. Mary had specifically told me not to bring anything electronic to the house. The squad cars arrived before Mary and Arthur could get the rug out undetected, so they left it behind. They figured any odor would be attributed to the blood in Mary's room. The threat of having an architect come in made it imperative that Mary get the rug out before someone tore into the wall and discovered it. She couldn't keep herself from paying Eileen one last, fatal visit while she was at it. After all, she felt it was Eileen's harassment and the threat of losing the house and her fortune that forced her to liquidate the estate and to leave. She knew if she stayed, Eileen would have found a way to take it all away."

"I had trouble believing she'd come back," Nicholls admitted. "She'd gotten away with the money."

"You don't know Mary," Eileen said. "You don't know how important winning is to that woman. She wanted me to suffer."

"And she couldn't afford to be found out," Jennifer added. "Besides, as far as she was concerned, her trip back was perfectly safe. She was convinced everyone thought she was dead, and she had no reason to believe anyone was aware of the passages."

"How do you think she found them?" Sam asked.

"She must have been determined to discover how Juliet was slipping in and out of the house. The tunnel's existence only confirmed her fears that Juliet was sleeping with Malcolm."

"Until you told me, I had no idea that Juliet had had an abortion," Eileen confessed.

"Of course you didn't. Mary helped her hide it, but Melba and Luther suspected she was pregnant, as did Mary. She probably suffered from morning sickness. But neither of them told Shelby, and when Juliet killed herself—"

"They carried the guilt," Sam finished.

Jennifer nodded.

"And how do you think Juliet found the passageways?" Sam asked.

"If you lock someone in a room enough times, and there's a way out, they'll find it," Jennifer assured him.

"Is this relevant?" Nicholls asked.

"Probably not to you."

"But how did you get the word to Mary?" Eileen asked. "How did you get her to come back?"

"With a newspaper article that Sam wrote," Jennifer explained. "We had copies delivered to Arthur's home and to his grandfather's house. I knew Luther read the newspapers every day. He told me. And I knew he would tell Arthur about what had happened with you, just in case he didn't read it for himself. We gave Mary the Monday deadline with the architect so she'd have to strike this weekend. And, of course, she did."

Eileen sighed. "And now we have Shelby's will, too."

"Right," Jennifer agreed.

"Where was it found?" Sam asked.

"Tucked in a hollow piece of molding," Nicholls told him. "Once we figured out the kind of trip mechanism used for the passage entrances, it wasn't all that hard to find. I'm sure he planned to let someone know where it was before he died."

"Mary never let any of us alone with him," Eileen assured him. "But it's over now, and everything has been set right."

Almost everything.

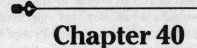

# Chapter 40

"... and you should leave out that whole subplot about the asteroid," Jennifer heard April telling Leigh Ann. "When writing about cataclysmic events, the romance *has* to take a backseat, so I suggest you either . . ."

"Just listen to her," Teri whispered loudly. She was leaning against the wall in Monique's kitchen, her eyes narrow, her arms crossed. "Now that she's going to be published, she thinks she knows everything. She doesn't write anything remotely similar to what Leigh Ann and I do, yet she told me to change the title of *Deep Frozen Love* and to move my story to New York City. My heroine trains sled dogs in the wilds of Alaska, for Heaven's sake! She hasn't seen a human for six months when she finds Ramon almost dead on the ice and takes him in and . . . Well, you've read it. And then she said, 'Of course she falls in love with him. Anything without long ears and a tail would look pretty good to her after nothing but snow.'

"I even heard her telling Monique to write a romance," Teri went on, "because, according to April, they're easier to sell. Hah! Can you imagine what kind of romance Monique would write? Some kind of slimy alien—argh! It makes me ill just thinking about it."

Jennifer nodded. The dark god of publishing had

**219**

struck again and created one more monster. "She'll get over it." At least she hoped she would.

"I don't know . . ." Teri batted a balloon out of the way. They were tied everywhere: to the chairs, the drawer pulls on the cabinets, even the light fixture. "If she gets a contract for more of these Billy and Barney books, and it looks like she will, we may get to know an April we never knew existed."

Monique drew a long knife from a drawer and handed it to April. "Time to cut your cake."

It was huge, four layers of rich chocolate frosted with cream cheese icing, sitting in the middle of the table next to a vase full of pink roses. It was one of Dee Dee's most popular sellers. *Way to Go, April!* was written in swirled red and pink icing.

Teri scowled and Jennifer punched her arm. "Be good. If we're lucky, this will happen to all of us one day and you'll get your turn to be Mr. Hyde."

April put down the knife, her eyes glistening. "I want to thank all of you. I never could have done it without you." She could as easily have been accepting an academy award. "Jennifer's suggestion to make Billy older and change Barney from a bat to a flying squirrel made all the difference. Monique's constant encouragement, Leigh Ann's line editing, and Teri's help with the plot. . . . This book is every bit as much your success as it is mine."

Jennifer glanced at Teri who promptly lowered her eyes.

"I love every one of you." Her voice cracked. "I'm the second, but I can't wait for the rest of you to get published!"

Jennifer knew that she meant it. It was hard to handle, the tears of joy that they all shared and that tiny ache she knew was in each of their hearts, wanting so much to be the next. She knew that April felt that ache as well.

"Group hug!" Leigh Ann called out, spreading her arms wide. They all crowded together, even Monique.

"Enough," Monique directed, pulling back and wiping tears from her eyes. "We've got cake to eat."

April cut five pieces, each large enough to supply an entire day's ration of calories for an adult female, and Leigh Ann scooped gobs of vanilla ice cream on top.

"So what happens to Arthur?" Teri leaned close.

"Probably very little." Jennifer handed April the plate with the first piece cut, then offered one to Teri before taking one for herself. "As far as he knew, he was simply helping Mary disappear with her own money. He probably didn't believe what he was doing should have been illegal."

"Do you think he would have stood by and let Mrs. McEvoy go to prison for murder?" Teri asked. She dipped her finger in some icing and tasted it. "Man, this is good."

"Of course it is," Jennifer assured her. "It's Dee Dee's own recipe. I hope he wouldn't, but who knows. Mary paid him really well, a heck of a lot more than that $10,000 he added to his account here. The police found an offshore account with a quarter of a million dollars in it and there may be more in other accounts."

"Whoa! I know a whole lot of people who'd do a lot more than he did for that amount of money. Did he plant the knife in Eileen's garden?"

"I suspect Mary did it before she left town, at least that's what Arthur's saying. She seems so out of it, she can't even be questioned."

"Yeah, right."

"But if Mary did do it, Arthur had to realize it was her. He knew about the notes that Mary had written and wanted me to pass off as threats. When he came to my apartment and fixed me lunch—"

"Get out of here! You didn't tell me that."

"He was there to make sure I'd played my part, given the police the notes, and then he told me my work was finished. But something he said that day stuck in the back of my mind. I knew something was wrong, but I couldn't figure out exactly what it was."

"What do you mean?"

"He told me I'd done what Mary *paid* me to do, but I never told him that Mary had given me money. As to whether or not he knew at that point how far Mary planned to go to frame Eileen, I doubt we'll ever know. He'd be an idiot to confess. He was fine with letting Eileen be suspected of murder, even with ruining her reputation. It's hard to say exactly when he would have said enough is enough."

"Mmmmm. It's difficult. Once you make that choice to be silent," Teri said, "speaking up just gets harder and harder."

"Is this a private conversation or can anyone join?" Leigh Ann put her arms around their necks and stuck her head between theirs. "What I want to know is how you explain the ghost sightings."

"All I can do is speculate," Jennifer said, "but we know Mary used the lantern when she came through the passageways. If the light was seen from the street by someone with an overactive imagination, he or she might believe it was Amy haunting the house."

"Well, you haven't convinced me it wasn't Amy Loggins, like the book says," Leigh Ann insisted, stubborn as always.

"She just made your case," Teri said.

Leigh Ann swatted at her and then hugged them both tight. "It's down to the three of us, my friends."

"Yep," Teri agreed. "April's deserted us for the land of the published."

"She's right, isn't she?" Leigh Ann asked. "We'll all get published one day, won't we?"

"One day," Jennifer promised. If they all lived long enough.

# Epilogue

Eileen had asked Jennifer to come to the mansion and help her pack up Juliet's belongings. She couldn't get rid of any of them, not yet, but it was time they were out of that room, time Juliet's memory was put to rest. Melba couldn't bring herself to help, and Eileen didn't feel right asking Monique.

When Eileen had stepped out of the room to get them both some iced tea, Jennifer found a small volume behind Juliet's dresser. Attempting to retrieve a barrette that had fallen behind it, she had discovered the volume pushed to the far back corner next to the leg.

She'd taken it, shamelessly, without a word to Eileen, and tucked it into her pocket. Alone in her apartment, Jennifer ran her fingers over the leather volume stamped with the word *Diary*. She opened the cover and flipped through the pages searching for the last entry. She was violating Juliet's privacy for the final time. "I promise," she whispered to herself. "No more."

The date read October 13, 1972.

*Malcolm must think I hate him. We said such horrible things to each other. Once I've done what I'm planning, he will have to somehow know that it's not because of him or anything he said to me, not because of his anger. It's because of me, of what I did. It was*

*my decision to make, not Mary's. It was me who didn't*
*have the courage to tell her no.*

*I asked the doctor if he could tell what sex the baby*
*would have been. He said it was a boy. Our little*
*Darren.*

*Please forgive me, Malcolm. I will always love you.*
                                                      *Juliet*

Jennifer closed the book, an overwhelming sadness en-
gulfing her once more. She went to her desk, and, from
the left hand drawer, dug out a padded envelope. She
slipped the diary inside, and sealed the flap. Across the
front she wrote *Malcolm Reed*. Then she copied the post
office box number from the copy of the free paper that
Monique had left with her.

She was not going to allow Mary to control the rest of
Malcolm's life. He had to know he wasn't the reason
Juliet committed suicide.

She felt something tickle the back of her neck, and she
whirled. But it was only an unexpected breeze coming
through the window. She turned back and listened to it
whistle through the leaves outside. Surely she only imagined she heard *thank you*.

# DYING TO GET EVEN

## by Judy Fitzwater

When Jennifer Marsh finds the body of the reprehensible owner of Edgar's Down Home Grill, she also catches Emmie, his ex-wife and her dear friend, nearby, gripping a bloody knife. Knowing that Emmie could never kill anyone, Jennifer and her writers' critique group join forces to figure out who's been plotting murder.

"In DYING TO GET EVEN are the seeds of a very funny parody of genre writing. . Jennifer and her friends are a genial bunch—and one can't help but root for them."

—*Rock Hill Herald* (SC)

# DYING FOR A CLUE

## by Judy Fitzwater

**To obtain some real-life investigative experience, Jennifer joins a private eye on an assignment. But when their late-night rendezvous explodes into murder, Jennifer finds herself high on the killer's hit list.**

"DYING FOR A CLUE is a fast-paced, easy read that is entertaining and beguiling. No matter the genre, anyone who is an aspiring writer will identify with Jennifer and find her 'writing' situations remarkably familiar."

—*Romantic Times*

**Published by Fawcett Books.**
**Available at your local bookstore.**

# DYING TO REMEMBER

## by Judy Fitzwater

Jennifer Marsh's high school reunion is truly a nightmare. All that's needed to make the evening a complete disaster is murder—an oversight soon gruesomely remedied by person or persons unknown. Trapped in the dangerous thick of it is Jennifer, knowing too much to suit a killer . . . and dying to remember enough to save her own life.

"Fitzwater comes through with an imaginative plot, hilarious secondary characters (the critique group, mostly aspiring romance writers, is a hoot) and good red herrings to throw readers off the track."

—*Publishers Weekly*

**Published by Fawcett Books.
Available at your local bookstore.**

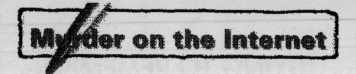